LIFE
Unworthy of

BY

DEREK ELKINS

WWW.LIFEUNWORTHY.COM

PUBLISHED BY

ATHANATOS
PUBLISHING GROUP

Life Unworthy of Life
   by Derek Elkins

Published by Athanatos Publishing Group
Copyright 2013
All Rights Reserved

ISBN 978-1-936830-48-0

Book website:
www.lifeunworthy.com

Publisher website:
www.athanatosministries.org

Cover Design by Julius Broqueza

About the Cover:

   This is a view from within the Holocaust Museum near the Brandenburg Gate in Germany, not very far from the bunker where the Third Reich finally fell with Hitler's suicide.

To God and my wife
who have always believed in me.

On September 1, 1939, Adolph Hitler authorized a program
Of euthanasia and eugenics called Action T4.
That program would eventually end the lives of over
200,000 mentally and physically handicapped Germans.

LIFE
Unworthy of

BY

DEREK ELKINS

WWW.LIFEUNWORTHY.COM

PUBLISHED BY

ATHANATOS
PUBLISHING GROUP

CHAPTER ONE

Dieter Himmelbach stared out the third floor window of the sanitarium into the cold autumn dusk. Below him, the trees had already turned and dropped a portion of their dead, to be blown to other sites by a bitter wind.

The gentle calling of "medications, medications" rang over the loud speaker, causing Dieter to raise his sightless eyes and smile ever so slightly.

Martin, the young schizophrenic who played solitaire continuously next to the window, threw his cards down violently onto the cardboard table and leapt to his feet. "About time, too," he said as he turned to Dieter. "Come along, Moon, it's feeding time."

Dieter hesitated by the window.

"Well, what are you waiting for, darling," Martin asked, as he proffered his arm. "If you don't take my arm, I'll find some pretty young fraulein who will."

"Sure you will," answered Dieter.

Dieter felt Martin come to a stop and knew that they stood in the line for medication. Louisa, that Spanish beauty who laughed uncontrollably at every odd noise, would be in front of them and Helt, the eight-year-old who grunted would be pulling up caboose.

"All right, Moon," said Martin, "We're in the station and about to be removed from existence."

"Don't call him Moon," said Louisa. "It's not funny."

Helt, from behind and slightly to the left, grunted in agreement, causing Louisa to break out in hysterical gales. Nevertheless, the merriment was short-lived.

"Louisa!" The sharp crack of Gerhardine's voice came from somewhere down the line and all grew silent.

Martin broke the silence with an exaggerated stage whisper. "Oh no, Moon, look at that. The Gestapo's here tonight. They must have come for you. You better run while you can, Moon, before they take you away forever and ever, before they lock you up and flush the key down the Fürher's trousers."

"Shut up, Martin" Louisa whispered back. "You know that's not funny."

Martin leaned in closer. "You know what I overheard the other day, Moon? I heard our precious Herr Bram state that we're all being moved to a work camp later this week. Apparently the Reich is tired

1

of keeping us in rice pudding and needs the extra money for the war effort. They decided to turn us all into glue."

Helt grunted and Louisa giggled, biting it off quickly. They must have been getting close to where Nurse Gerhardine doled out the evening's pharmaceuticals.

"Louisa," came the stilted voice of Nurse Gerhardine somewhere close by.

"Ma'am," Louisa answered just as stiffly as Martin and Dieter stepped closer.

Martin dropped Dieter's elbow as he moved to take his pills.

"Martin," said Nurse Gerhardine. "Have you been behaving yourself today?"

"Yes, Ma'am," said Martin.

"I would hate to have to put you in the room again," she said. "I know how you desperately hate that dark, cold room, so far away from the others."

"Yes, Ma'am," Martin said.

"Well, go on, then."

Martin stepped off and Dieter moved in front of the window.

"Oh, and what do we have here?" Nurse Gerhardine asked. "Why, it's our little moon calf. Found anything to talk about today, moon calf?"

Always she asked and always he replied with silence.

"Here are your oats," she repeated for the thousandth time and thrust a small cup of pills into Dieter's waiting hands. Dieter moved three steps and stopped, waiting for Martin to guide him again.

Martin grabbed Dieter's arm and began to lead him to the radio room when he was stopped by some loud excitement.

"You there," Nurse Gerhardine yelled. "Get away from that window, all of you."

"What is it?" Dieter asked.

"I don't know," Martin answered. "Hold on."

In a moment, the Dieter's friend had returned. "I don't know what's going on," he said, "but there are three buses parked out front and they look like they belong to the government. Maybe we are being moved to a work camp."

A half an hour later, the excitement began to wear thin as the boys and girls went about their scheduled routines. Soon, it was time for bed and Martin led Dieter to the dormitory they shared with fourteen other boys. There was no time for play as they were hustled

2

into their state-issued pajamas and the light was abruptly extinguished at nine o'clock.

While the other boys settled down to sleep, the pills made any roughhousing a non-existence, Dieter used the time in the second darkness to pray for his family.

* * * * * *

It seemed that he'd been asleep for only a few minutes when Dieter was jostled awake by the sound of the dormitory door crashing into the wall. Nurse Gerhardine's voice rang out harshly through the small room.

"Wake up, boys! Wake up right now! Get out of bed and get to your feet this instant!"

Dieter, along with the other boys, staggered to his feet, leaning against the bed frame for support. Midnight inspections were not unusual, but they had just had one a few days ago. There shouldn't have been another one so soon unless something had been stolen again.

"Put your hands out!" Nurse Gerhardine commanded.

A cloth sack was placed in Dieter's waiting hands.

"You will immediately get dressed and place all of your remaining belongings into the sack you were just issued. Then you will stand in front of your bunks until you are told to do otherwise."

Dieter, along with the other boys hurried to comply with the instructions. The nurses and orderlies made sure that hesitation to follow orders was strictly punished. They worked in silence because work was always completed in silence.

After a moment, all the boys had completed the assignment; most had only a few articles of clothing to their names, and were standing at the foot of their bunks. Martin touched Dieter's arm reassuringly as Nurse Gerhardine barked out again.

"Now you're all going to board a bus. You're moving to a new hospital."

This announcement was met with chaos. Several boys broke out in hurried conversations and one small boy, Herman, began to cry.

"Shut up! Shut your faces right now!" Nurse Gerhardine commanded and the boys obeyed. "There will be no more talking for this point forward."

The boys were soon moving through the hallways and stairwells of the sanitarium. The only sounds came from their whispering feet, the occasional sack full of clothes brushing against a wall and the

3

soft sobbing of some boy, probably Herman. They came to a final door that, when opened, released a blast of pre-winter wind full upon the boys. Nearby, Dieter could hear diesel engines revving slightly.

Luckily, Martin had remained close to Dieter and was able to lead him forward into the night's chill. Dieter could hear the voice of Herr Bram, a counselor, speaking urgently with what had to be a guard or an officer of the Reich.

"But you can't move these children without explaining to their parents and caretakers what happened to them. They'll be missed and we'll have to deal with it."

A polished voice answered him. "Don't worry about things best left to others, Doctor Bram. You just do your job, like a good German citizen and we'll let the SS handle the explanations. This is a government-run facility, isn't it?"

"Well, yes, but Captain Oster..."

"But nothing, Herr Bram. You just let the government handle these..." He struggled for a word, "these unmentionables and we'll send you scores of wounded and damaged heroes to attend to instead. These patients are now part of the T4 program and are beyond your concern. Now, isn't that a more satisfying solution?"

"Satisfying for whom?" Came the response, but Dieter was soon out of earshot and hustled aboard a freezing, smoke-filled bus. Martin didn't speak until they were seated, and then only in hushed tones.

"I don't know what's going on, Moon, but it looks as if they're moving us to a different facility. There must have been a dozen soldiers out in the courtyard. They probably found out about your secret alliance and are shipping you off to Siberia. I can't figure out for the life of me why they're taking the rest of us though."

Suddenly, there was a commotion in the courtyard. Dieter could hear several voices raised: one of them clearly the officer previously speaking to Bram. The other one...

"It's that kid, Planck, the one who got sent to the room five times last week for crying for his mother over and over again during radio time."

Dieter nodded, remembering how Planck had started weeping several times after the program they had been listening to had mentioned a mother. Something hard had hit the west wall and then Planck had started screaming about how they had taken his mother away from him and how he would never see her again.

Dieter's thoughts were broken suddenly by a loud crack, almost as if the truck's tire had blew, which was followed immediately by Martin's sharp intake of breath. Then the screaming and shouting took over. Dieter knew that the shrill screaming had to be Gerhardine. He had heard that high-pitched sound so often in the night. But the shouting...

Suddenly a man's voice came from the front of the bus. "Mac schnell. Get moving!"

The doors to the bus slammed shut and it took off.

Martin was shaking. "They shot him. They shot him."

A woman's voice, one he had never heard before, came from up near the driver. "Calm down now, children! I said calm down! Now, whatever you think you saw, you didn't. Everyone is fine. The truck simply backfired. No need to worry about that other boy. He'll be just fine."

Some, but not all calmed down a bit, as evidenced by the reduced whispering and soft crying. Martin continued to shake, but canceled his litany.

The nurse continued, "Now, we'll be on this trip for a little over two hours. I suggest you get back to sleep as soon as you can. There'll be no bathroom stops. There'll be no stops for food. I don't entertain troublemakers on my bus. If you cause me any grief during this short trip, you'll be punished swiftly. We'll arrive at our destination shortly."

The nurse, or whatever she was, became quiet and silence reigned on the small bus.

After a few moments, Martin put his lips close to Dieter's ear and whispered, "I've never seen anyone killed before, but I know that wasn't backfire from a bus. People don't fall to the ground and spurt blood from their heads from backfire. At least I don't think so."

A few seconds passed before Martin spoke once more. "I don't mind telling you, Moon: I'm scared. I don't know what's going on, but whatever it is, it's not good."

And mercifully, Martin became silent, allowing Dieter time to think.

* * * * * *

"All right, children," the nurse said, "it's time to wake up. We've reached your new home."

At the first spoken word, Martin was instantly awake. "We're in a

5

courtyard, Moon," Martin whispered. "Some kind of castle. There are men in white coats waiting along with some more soldiers. I don't know what crime you committed this time, Moon, but it must have been something."

They were all moved off the bus after grabbing their sparse belongings and positioned in a row on the cold cobblestone entryway. The silence and cold lingered for a few agonizing moments before being interrupted by a slightly seasoned German voice.

"Former residents of Hospital 5512, Strassberg. Welcome to your new home. This is the castle Zarfuyls. The lovely village you passed on the long trek up the mountain was Sterlingaart, for any of you interested in geography.

"While residing here, you will be in the presence of some of the most respected and able physicians the Fatherland has to offer. You will be cared for. The food is superb, the countryside is magnificent. You will find rest and recuperation here.

"But we do have rules, ladies and gentlemen. And we expect these rules to be obeyed at any and all times. If a staff member gives you instruction, you are expected to obey that instruction immediately and purposefully. Rude and malicious behavior will not be tolerated.

"There are many other items to go over, but tonight is not the best time for such as those. Simply obey the staff and your time here will go smoothly and painlessly. I hope you all relish the fact that you were all chosen to participate in the T4 program, the Reich's shining star."

The man paused, to allow his words to float to the ground, before continuing. "My name is Dr. Obermayer and I am in charge of this operation. All staff report to me. Now, boys and girls, you will be shown to your dormitories."

Martin gently guided Dieter forward as the line began to move. Soon, they had all passed the great wooden entryway of Castle Zarfuyls and were swallowed by its presence.

CHAPTER TWO

The taxi halted directly in front of a simple house in a poorly lit area of Sterlingaart. As the cab seemed to have no intention of moving further, Viktor Gottlieb hesitantly peered through the window at the unfriendly parish house with its darkened windows and shadow-swept front lawn. There was no sign of warmth here, except for the single plume of smoke that escaped the chimney.

"This is it," the driver prompted.

Viktor shook his head and turned his attention to the front of the cab. "Of course. And how much do I owe you?"

In the mirror, the cab driver's eyes shifted over the top of Viktor's suit coat and expensively groomed hair. Viktor could almost visualize the driver mentally cranking up his intended fare to account for the passenger.

"That'll be 15 Reich marks, Herr Doctor."

Viktor stopped himself before the argument ever approached his lips. The price didn't matter, at least when it was being covered by the government. Viktor pulled the amount from his wallet and handed it to the driver.

Swiftly, Viktor opened the door and allowed the cold air access to his face. As soon as he had shut the door, the cab sped away, leaving Viktor in blackness.

He could just make out the shape of the church next door to the parish. It wasn't much, by any city's standards. Viktor had seen churches in Berlin so massive that they could have used this one as a confessional. But, then again, his brother had never been the one to yearn for the finer things in life. He had never been ambitious.

Yanking his coat closer to his body, Viktor stepped through the yard and toward the front door of the parish.

After his second knock, raised slightly louder than the first into a pounding, Viktor heard some action from within the confines of the house. A light shot on in one of the rooms, flooding the porch.

"Hold on, Father," came a voice from inside, "I'll be right there."

Viktor heard the latch withdraw and the door began to open.

"I didn't realize I had bolted…" The woman's voice began and stopped as soon as she got a look at the visitor on her doorstep.

A rather plump woman in robe and slippers scrutinized Viktor quickly. Before he had a chance to wonder if he had made a mistake, the woman addressed him.

"I'm sorry, but Father Gottlieb isn't home at the moment."

"Not at home?" Viktor questioned. "But it's Saturday night. Where on earth could he be?"

The woman opened her mouth and then shut it as quickly, peering at him suspiciously. "I'm sorry. Was the Father expecting you?"

Viktor smiled slightly. "No, he wasn't expecting me. But he'll be happy to see me, I'm sure. I'm his brother, Viktor."

Realization bloomed on her face like the sun rising, transforming her suspicion into a beatific smile. "His brother? Why, I'll be painted special. I didn't know Father August was expecting you. Of course, if he was, why would he tell me?" She took a moment to sweep over his face and clothes as if taking a mental picture.

"Do you mind if I come in while we wait?" Viktor asked.

The door swung widely open. "Oh, of course. Where are my manners? Please."

She ushered Viktor through a sitting room, overflowing with muted light and warmth, past a tiny kitchen and into what could only be a study, as it was lined near to overflowing with books, had numerous stuffed chairs and was bullied by a massive oak desk.

"My apologies again. I'm Senta, Father August's, I mean Father Gottlieb's housemaid. I clean up for him, do his laundry, all that needs to be done."

"Of course," remarked Viktor, as his eyes rolled over the books of a nearby shelf. "I'm sure a parish priest is much too busy to clean his house and iron his own socks."

The sarcasm was lost on Senta.

"Of course. He'd never get a thing accomplished if it wasn't for me and the other ladies of the church."

Apparently, thought Viktor, his brother had gone from his mother's house to a new home full of mothers. How fitting.

Senta must have been running full steam as her mouth refused to stop, even as she rushed out of the room. "Oh, and I'll get you some tea, shall I? Of course, it's a cold night out there. Cold enough to raise the dead, was what my mother used to say, but she was always a superstitious old coot. Never could get a lick of sense out of that woman. Ah, but she meant well, she did."

Senta burst into the study again with a cup of tea, which she thrust on the table next to one of the over-stuffed chairs. "Now, you take a sip of that, Viktor, if I may call you Viktor, and that'll take an edge off the cold soon enough."

Viktor barely glanced at the cup as his eyes were soon fixed to a trumpet that lay casually on its side on the desk.

"Tell me," said Viktor. "Does he still play that old thing?"

"Well, of course," Senta answered. "He'd play it morning, noon and night if I gave him the chance. But, it's odd that no matter how often or long he plays at that thing, it still comes out sounding like a sick cow."

Viktor chuckled despite himself.

Suddenly, the front door banged open.

"Oh, and that'll be the Father now. Please have a seat and I'll let him know you're here."

Senta moved off down the hall, leaving Viktor alone in the study. As his eyes roamed the bookshelf, Viktor was easily able to catch the conversation coming slowly his way down the hall.

"Oh, Father, isn't it wonderful?" Senta asked. "It isn't like you've seen him all these many years and here he is. And he's looking so good as well. I think the college must have scrubbed some of his boyhood right out of his life, but the clear Sterlingaart air surely brought it..."

"Slow down, Senta," came the voice of his brother, August. "What are you jabbering on about? Who has come for a visit?"

"Ah, but didn't I tell you," she answered. "Your brother Viktor arrived less than an hour ago. He's been waiting in the study."

"The study?" August exclaimed. "My brother? But I thought..."

Viktor smiled to himself at the imagined look of annoyance on his brother's face. He remembered how little August enjoyed surprises.

"Come along, Father. You haven't seen him in so long. Mustn't keep your brother waiting."

Viktor turned to the nearest chair and lay limply down, waiting for the arrival of his brother.

And then, without warning, his younger brother, August, looking slightly unkempt and like a college professor, with small spectacles adorning his face and hair untamed by the wind stood in the doorway. Unlike Viktor's blond hair, which was chopped close: close enough to meet Army regulations, which was, of course, the way the hospitals preferred their doctors to look, August's was dark as a midnight sky.

Viktor did not rise to meet his brother. A smile, however, swam across his face, not quite rising to meet his ice-chip blue eyes.

"Hello August," said Viktor.

August, still in temporary shock, moved slowly toward the table.

August pointed at the cup of tea in front of Viktor. "Can I get a cup of tea as well?" he asked Senta, who was occupying a position in the doorway.

"Of course, Father," Senta said. "Right away."

Senta departed as August sat in the chair reserved for those being counseled, opposite his brother. They took a moment, but just a moment, to refresh their memories and fill in the blanks before August broke the awkward silence.

"So, you look well," August said. "I see you survived the university life intact. And apparently your internship as well."

"Two grueling years in Berlin," said Viktor.

"Why, it's practically the edge of the world."

"It was hardly that," Viktor said. "Although it presented its own peculiar difficulties. The internship served its purpose. I broadened my contacts and enlarged my future."

"Did you now?" August asked. "So, now the accomplished doctor has persevered through his internship and is now voyaging around…Sterlingaart. Ah yes. The glorious vacationland that is Sterlingaart. What rich, promising doctor wouldn't set his sights here?"

Viktor smiled to himself. "You always did have more than your share of sarcasm, August. Got it from mother. Are you sure that it isn't some sort of sin?"

"Don't talk to me of sins, Viktor. What you did to mom: that was a sin."

Viktor's brow furrowed more in concentration than in concern. "What I did…"

"Yes. I can't tell you how many tear-stained letters I've had to pour over from our dear mother, agonizing because her brilliant doctor son doesn't have the time or energy to write to his lonely mother. I can't tell you how many long, Sunday afternoons I've had to spend consoling the woman who gave birth to you because she felt her oldest had forgotten all about her, leaving her for dead."

A genuine smile reached Viktor's eyes. "I thought that was what brilliant young doctors were supposed to do: part of the final exam, so to speak."

"And what about poor, parish priests," August asked. "Think all we have time to do is pacify our heartbroken mothers when their favorites no longer come to call?"

""What else do you have to do?" countered Viktor. "Don't you just wrestle with God all day? Surely, you can take a break and console a widow now and then? Or won't your busy schedule allow that much?"

August rose to his feet, a gaping smile spreading across his face. "Wrestle with God all day? Is that all I do?"

Viktor rose as well. "Well, I'm sure you have to speak your homilies as well...or count the money...or sing your mournful hymns over and over. It's not as if you have a real job."

"Real job?"

August good-naturedly lunged at Viktor from across the table as the two men began wrestling in the study. Viktor, the one in obvious better shape had the priest in a headlock and was backing him toward the door. At that moment, Senta entered, bearing a tray full of hot tea and crackers, which was immediately knocked from her hands.

"Oh, Father Gottlieb," Senta cried, stopping their match. "Really!"

Pausing to look at Senta, who was drenched with tea and covered in crackers, the brothers broke out laughing, which only served to bring a quiver to the maid's lower lip. August went immediately to her aid, sweeping her up in a hug.

"Oh, Senta," said August. "We're sorry."

"Very sorry," confirmed Viktor, now on the other side of the desk, as if to distance himself from the situation.

"And we'll never do it again," said August.

Senta released herself firmly from the priest's grip and straightened her back, as if properness could cleanse her from the situation. "I should hope not. Two respectable gentlemen such as yourselves acting like overgrown school boys."

Released, August stepped over to where his brother now sat. The priest grabbed his brother's shoulder and squeezed. "But give us a bit of rope, Senta. After all, I haven't seen big brother Viktor in over five years."

"More like six actually," Viktor said.

Senta left the room with a scowl as August headed toward his seat. After getting comfortable, he re-started the conversation. "So? Sterlingaart?"

Viktor shrugged. He knew he'd have to offer the story sooner or later.

"Are you here for a visit," asked August, "or is it something a bit more permanent?"

Viktor pointed to a trumpet proudly displayed on the desk. "Are you still playing that old thing?"

"More like trying to wring its pitiful neck of anything resembling music. It keeps me busy. Are you evading the question?"

"I'll be here for a while," Viktor answered.

"Why? Berlin wasn't big enough for you?"

"Sterlingaart's big enough for my little brother. Why shouldn't it fit me as well?"

"Oh, come on, Viktor. I was assigned here. If the former parish priest hadn't been ninety-two, I wouldn't be here either. There's nothing further away from civilization than Sterlingaart. So why would one of the top ten graduates from the University of Berlin Medical School, a young scientist so promising that he was able to intern at the prestigious East Stutgard Hospital, and one of the fifty on the Führer's personal list ever want to be in the sleepy little hamlet of Sterlingaart? What could you possibly want or do here?"

"Actually," said Viktor, "that's an interesting story."

"I'll bet it is."

"The Führer's director of science and medicine, Philip Brand, requested me personally. Apparently the Reich is rolling out a new program and I'm to be involved."

"A new program?" August asked, with an interesting tinge to his voice.

"That's right," Viktor said. "I can't speak too much about it, but it weighs heavily in the Fatherland's future."

August dug into his pocket and threw a wadded up piece of paper on the table between the two of them. "Does this have anything to do with the secret project?"

Raising an eyebrow, Viktor carefully straightened out what was clearly a poster and took a moment to scrutinize it.

The poster featured a tiny, twisted human thing on a chair with a bright figure of the Reich's loyal order of health care standing behind. The caption read, "60,000 Reich marks is what this person suffering from a hereditary disease costs the people's community during his lifetime. Comrade, that is your money too. Read, 'A New People', the monthly magazine for the Bureau for Race Politics of the NSDAP."

"Crude," Viktor said. "But it gets the point across."

"And what point is that: that Germany can only move forward if we get rid of its dead weight first?"

"Oh come off your cloud, August. You know as well as I do that we can't keep emptying the coffers of Germany to support those who'll never lead a full life anyway. Not when we need the money to take care of the Fatherland's real heroes: the soldiers who risk their lives every day. War is here. The Reich needs to free up every deutschmark available or we're going to lose. We can't allow the dregs of our land to soak the supply line when it's needed the most."

August sat silent for a moment. "So, the solution is to exterminate those societal leeches that are sucking the monetary lifeblood from Germany?"

Viktor smiled and slowly shook his head. "Still listening to all the rumors, eh brother? I know there's a lot of talk about ethnic cleansing and secret murders. But this program doesn't have anything to do with that. We started out with some sterilizations. That's true. But now we're moving forward. Look, I worked in the long-term disability ward at East Stutgard. I saw exactly how God's little precious ones were treated by those who supposedly loved them. For most of them, it would've been better if they were never born."

"Just because there were a few…"

Viktor held up his hand. "No. Now listen for once. There was a little boy that had been on the ward for several months named Frans: just a little boy, no older than seven or eight. He had suffered from Spinal Meningitis from the day he was born. His mother was a prostitute and his father was a drunk. He was in incredible pain, day and night. When he was first brought in, he had bruises all over his body where his parents had severely beaten him. Apparently, they couldn't stand his screams of pain, so they were beating him to silence. I learned later that they had kept him in a cage for the last several months."

August, looking down at his hands, answered finally. "The Bible tells us that there's sin in the world…"

"Yes, it does," Viktor said. "And possibly the greatest sin is forcing someone to live when all they really want is death."

"Is that what Frans wanted," August whispered, "to die?"

Viktor looked off, sudden tears at the rim of his eyes. "Oh, there

13

were days when he would beg me to end his life. Have you ever looked into the eyes of pain, tears streaming down the cheeks, as a little boy begged you to put him out of his misery?"

"And, are you the one who decides who lives and who dies?" August asked. "Did God grant you the responsibility to make that determination?"

Viktor stood up abruptly. "No, the Führer did. Now, I'm afraid I must be off. I've got to get settled."

August stood as well, the debate temporarily halted. "Look, don't go yet. Where are you staying?"

"I'll be staying at the local psychiatric hospital, now operating out of Zarfuyls Castle. But for now, I'm staying in a room at the White Stag tavern. They haven't renovated the doctor's rooms yet. I was heading over there now as soon as I said hello to my little brother."

August reached out, grabbed Viktor's shoulder. "Look, let's forget all the arguments for now. There'll be plenty of time for theological discussions and talks in the future. After all, you won't be too far away. But, stay here tonight."

Viktor frowned. "Ah, I'd love to, August, but the Führer's already paid for the room…"

August's hand gently eased him back into the chair. "Now, we both know that you won't be charged if you don't stay tonight. Besides, I know the man who owns that inn. I'll talk to him for you."

Viktor smiled over the top of his cup. "Ah, the privileges of the priestly class."

August laughed suddenly. "Privileges? Right. Oh, there's privileges certainly. I get to stay up late with grieving parents and clean up after alcoholics. I get to console widows and orphans. Those are my privileges." August bent forward toward his brother. "Say, do me a favor? Stay the night tonight and stay for service tomorrow."

Viktor's eyes threatened to roll into the back of his skull. "Oh, I'd really love to stay for your service. I mean that. It's just…"

"Now, now," replied August. "There's no cause to making a great production over the whole thing. This isn't mom and dad forcing you to attend. You're an adult now. Surely you can stand one service and listen to your dear baby brother give a nice homily. After all, it would make our saintly, old mother so proud to see her oldest in

14

church finally."

Viktor knew when he was being pushed but he didn't care. "Our saintly old mother? And will she be there tomorrow?"

"As a matter of fact..."

"Okay," said Viktor. "May as well get two uncomfortable situations out of the way at once. That way, you can't say that I never attended one of your boring services and I'll get the meeting with mother over as well. I can't say I'm looking forward to tomorrow, though."

"Well, thank you very much," said August.

As the night continued, their talks returned to more social and political matters.

CHAPTER THREE

The next day, Viktor awoke to some very strange woman shaking him by the shoulder. Half in a daze, he slapped her hands away.

"How dare you," he slurred. "Where am I?"

Before she could answer, his eyes took in the surroundings and his head swam fully out of sleep. "Oh, of course. I'm sorry."

Senta's disapproving gaze said that it would take quite a while to forgive rudeness. "That's quite all right, Herr Gottlieb. Now, when you're fully roused, I have breakfast waiting in the kitchen."

Viktor raised himself up on one arm. "My brother?"

Senta paused at the door. "Father Gottlieb has been awake for some time now. Already eaten his breakfast and is now preparing himself at the church. Service begins in less than one hour."

And without another word, she left the room.

Viktor shook his head and hoped dearly that the housekeeper knew how to make a respectable pot of coffee.

* * * * * *

Viktor entered the sanctuary just as the crowd around him began to grow quiet. Just in time, Viktor congratulated himself.

He looked furtively around the congregation, with as many eyes pouring on him, and finally saw his mother halfway up the left row of pews. Her eyes said that she had seen him as soon as he had entered. He bowed his head as he moved past several others in her row and finally seated himself next to her.

He bent close to her. "Sorry, I'm late."

She reached over and took his hand, squeezing quickly. "It's good to see you, Viktor."

As the first chords on the organ were struck, she turned her eyes obediently toward the pulpit.

* * * * * *

The rhythms of the Mass marched forward, trampling the congregation in its path. At times, Viktor would look over and see the altar boy mouthing the words in synchronization with August. Yes, the boy would make a fine priest one day. They indoctrinated them young in the Catholic Church.

Viktor glanced over to his mother on several occasions, but her eyes were raptly held toward the front as if she were witnessing the

Savior Himself. Another mindless drone, entranced by the drug called religion. Well, she had always been that way. It had been father who had stopped attending once his sons were old enough to make up their own minds. But she had continued, at first to stay with August, or at least that's what she said. But Viktor knew, even back then. She may have been married to father but her real husband was the church.

The tones of Mass died down for a moment as August stepped behind the pulpit. He looked once to his left and nodded to another man, bald and spectacled, who stood behind the nearby lectern.

The man nodded back, as if to reassure himself, adjusted his spectacles and began to read the passage haltingly. "Listen, O isles, unto me; and hearken, ye people, from far; The LORD hath called me from the womb; from the bowels of my mother hath he made mention of my name. And he hath made my mouth like a sharp sword; in the shadow of his hand hath he hid me, and made me a polished shaft; in his quiver hath he hid me; And said unto me, Thou art my servant, O Israel, in whom I will be glorified. Then I said, I have labored in vain, I have spent my strength for naught, and in vain: yet surely my judgment is with the LORD, and my work with my God. And now, saith the LORD that formed me from the womb to be his servant, to bring Jacob again to him, Though Israel be not gathered, yet shall I be glorious in the eyes of the LORD, and my God shall be my strength."

As the man stumbled forward, Viktor took the time to glance around at the intent faces. It was always like this in rural areas, and especially in war. The intelligent turned to greater weapons and the peasants turned to God. It was said that war brings out the reality of death and that reality turns men to look after their own souls. Ah, but what would they say the moment they woke from death and found that they had been following a dream the whole time?

Quietly, and with great reverence, the bald man closed the Bible, backed away from the lectern and returned to a seat on the first row.

After the man seated himself, August began. "Do we, pitiful and broken humans that we are, have the right to decide the importance of individual human life?

"This question reaches the utmost importance in times such as these: times of war. When I have a weapon and I know that if I don't kill my enemy, then he will certainly kill me, that situation places me almost in the same realm as God. Ultimately, I am the one to decide who lives and dies. I can decide to whom I wish to extend grace, whom to be my prisoner and who I want to kill outright.

"In the same way, how society deals with their dangerous criminals affects questions on the death penalty. How do we make decisions in these situations and honor the supremacy of almighty God? How can we wrestle decisions such as these out of the hands of the One who made us, the One who knows tomorrow?"

Viktor knew exactly who was in charge when questions of life or death reared their ugly heads: The doctors, of course. They were the ones who gave life or allowed it to slip away. The days of miracle-working carpenters were long past, swallowed up by the stark reality of Evolution. In this age of reason, there was no time for miracles, no time to wait on a slow-moving and incoherent God who allowed some to live and some to die and who answered his followers' prayers only when he felt like it. If Viktor took the time for God to show up in his emergency room, the patient would be long gone.

August continued. "The Bible states that only God is the giver of life and, as such, is the only one authorized to take life. Jeremiah 29:11 states, 'For I know the thoughts that I think toward you, saith the Lord, thoughts of peace and not of evil, to give you an expected end.' Only God knows the future of any given life. We, as fallible human beings can guess on the outcome of a life, but our opinions are based on inferior knowledge. Just because a man may fall ninety-nine times, does not guarantee that the man will fall the hundredth. And just because a father has a drinking problem does not mean the son will as well."

Oh, and how about that as a solution to the legitimacy of a supreme being? If there was a God, why was there war in the first place? Why would he allow people, especially children to suffer and die at the hands of selfish and angry men? Why would a god that was good allow a drunk to beat his children to death? How could you even call a god that allowed such things to happen, "good"? Where was the justice, the humanity, in that?

"And what about the condition of a man?" August asked. "Are we God, where we can see the inside of a man and know his true worth? I may see a man who can no longer walk, but God may see a great teacher or a wonderful father. I may see a man who is blind, but God may see Claude Monet, the famous impressionist, or John Milton who authored Paradise Lost."

Apparently, his brother had allowed their conversation from last night to slip into his sermon preparation. He always had to get the last word in on any argument. Leave it to August to slip in the last word directly into his homily.

"I don't have the right to judge anyone because, as 1 Samuel 16:7 states, 'for the Lord seeth not as man seeth; for man looketh on the outward appearance, but the Lord looketh on the heart'. If I judge, I judge as a blind man. If I judge the worth of a man, I over-step my bounds."

Apparently, Viktor thought, God didn't look down far enough into men. If He did, He'd see what horrible, selfish destroyers He actually created.

* * * * * *

Viktor prepared himself. He knew that as soon as the service had ended and the crowd broken into their little jabbering cliques, his mother would begin hammering him about his lack of communication. He could almost sense her eagerness bursting over the top of her illusion of serenity.

So, he was a little at a loss when the service completed and his mother simply stood and motioned him toward the doors of the church. Silently, faithfully, just as his father had ingrained in him, Viktor followed his mother from the church.

At the doors stood August, like a bride-less groom at a wedding reception, shaking hands and exchanging words with his parishioners. The older couple directly in front of Viktor must have thought they were the last in line as they attempted to command the entire attention of the priest. Viktor's mother stood patiently, glancing through the trees and across the roofs of the town as Viktor leaned in closer to overhear their conversation.

"Father Gottlieb, you remember our son, Kolger?" the man asked.

"Of course," answered August, acknowledging his brother and mother's presence behind the older couple with a wink. "How could anyone forget Kolger?"

The old man pressed on. "As you know, or maybe you don't, we had been attempting to care for our young Kolger, although it is difficult and we receive little to no help from the state."

His wife broke in, "And it has been a struggle, father. As God is my witness. The boy means well, but he's always getting underfoot. He was getting…"

Suddenly, the old woman gave a harsh cry and broke into soft

19

sobbing. Viktor's mom moved forward quickly, hugging the woman's shoulders. "There, there, Maria," the boys' mother cooed. "It'll be all right."

Maria pushed Viktor's mother gently away. "I appreciate that, Elsa, but it won't be all right. No. Not any time soon."

The old man continued, ignoring the presence of Viktor's mother and Viktor. "We had been sending Kolger to Doctor Halls," August nodded at the name, "several times a week. And we had noticed some improvement in Kolger's behavior. Not much, mind you, but some still. Doctor Halls was trying to get the boy to favor his good foot and was working with him on his pronunciation. And then, as if night turned to day, Doctor Halls would no longer work with him."

Maria had regained enough to contribute. "Father, he said he was not allowed to work with Kolger anymore. He said he couldn't work with cripples any longer."

"Aye," agreed the old man. "We asked him where we could send Kolger and he just sent us away. It wasn't like him at all."

August assumed his pastoral smile. "Well, Gregor, Maria, that's not so bad. I think if we…" But the looks on their faces told him that the story was not quite finished. "What is it?"

Maria began to sob again, this time more quietly, as Gregor continued. "Late last Thursday night, we received a knock on our door. And, when we opened the door, who should be standing there but Doctor Halls, shoulder to shoulder with two members of the Schutzstaffel. They said they were part of some Reich Committee for the Scientific Registering of something or other. They took Kolger from my very house: the house I built with my own two hands. They entered my house and took my son."

It was the old man's turn to break down, leaving August in stunned silence. Viktor took the opportunity to step back and distance himself from the situation. It would only inflame matters if the old man and woman learned that he was working for the men that took their son away.

"Where…?" Viktor heard his brother say. "Did they say where they were taking him or why?"

Viktor was soon out of earshot and didn't hear the complete answer, but the name Castle Zarfuyls drifted up into the air above the grieving man and his wife.

* * * * * *

After saying goodbye to his brother, Viktor walked his mother back to her house in Sterlingaart. She explained that she had moved to be closer to August not soon after Viktor's father had died.

Viktor had feared her guilt for nothing, as she seemed to be empty of any bitterness. She just felt sorry that Viktor hadn't been in touch for so long and made him promise to see her now that he was living so close.

Viktor made certain to spare his mother any details of his new job assignment, as they would be sure to distress her at the very least. He instead entertained her with several short memories of his time as an intern in Berlin. Soon, they arrived at the door of her little cottage deep in the heart of Sterlingaart, which, as it turned out, was not very far from the White Stag Inn, where he would be staying temporarily.

As he moved to leave, Elsa Gottlieb grabbed hold of her son and brought him to her in a fierce hug. After a moment, Viktor hugged her back.

"Oh, Viktor, I'm so glad I have both of my boys near me once more." She whispered fiercely before releasing him.

* * * * * *

Kolger Fruskins had been in the specialized care of the doctors at Castle Zarfuyls for a week. They had poked and prodded him. They had asked him numerous questions about the hereditary nature of his clubfoot and cleft lip. Had anyone else in his family been born with a cleft lip? Did any of his maternal grandparents have a clubbed foot? Did he have any siblings with similar abnormalities?

All Kolger could do was repeatedly tell them that he was scared and wanted to go home. If they wanted to know about his family, they should ask his parents. He was tired and hungry and wanted to see his mother and father most of all. Why couldn't they just leave him alone and let him go home?

After repeating this line of questioning for a few days, the doctors involved reached a consensus on Kolger Fruskins.

On the Tuesday following his parents' meeting with August Gottlieb, Kolger was awakened and made to walk past the breakfast hall where the remainder of the patients ate a quiet and tasteless breakfast.

"I'm hungry," whined Kolger. "Can't we stop?"

The nurse who was leading him down the corridor shook her head. "I'm afraid not. The doctors said you were not allowed to eat the morning before your tests."

21

Kolger's face fell. "Not more tests. And why can't I eat? They let me eat before."

The nurse frowned. "Now, now. Mustn't cause trouble now. It's just until you've had your test. Then they'll let you eat."

Kolger was directed down one corridor and into an older area of the castle. There was no dust, however, even down this corridor. Everything was meticulously clean, just like a hospital. Finally, the nurse stopped in front of a heavy iron door. She rapped two times and listened. Apparently she heard something from within as a moment later she twisted the iron knob and opened the door.

The room featured a heavy wooden chair in its center, with an operating table and equipment set off to one side. The two doctors turned to greet Kolger with expansive smiles on their faces.

"Why if isn't young Kolger…" he looked down at the papers on the clipboard in front of him. "Young Kolger Fruskins. How wonderful to make your acquaintance. If you'll have a seat, we'll get started." As he turned to the nurse, all the play had slipped from his eyes. "You may leave."

The other "doctor" sat behind the desk and wrote furiously on a pad of paper as Kolger took the offered seat.

After the nurse left, the first doctor again turned to Kolger, his smile much too wide for his face. "So, it is just us now."

"Yes," answered Kolger, smiling faintly in response. "Uh, what kind of tests are we doing today?"

The doctor's smile slipped as he headed toward a covered tray. "Oh, we'll be taking some blood and giving you some steroids that should help you with your condition."

"Steroids?" Kolger asked. "What's that?"

The doctor removed the cloth from the tray, revealing five gleaming syringes, three of which were filled with an ochre mixture and the remaining two were empty. The doctor continued, as he slowly examined the syringes. "Steroids are special medicine that enhances the strength of your muscles and bones. They may just be the solution for a problem such as yours."

"My problem?" Kolger swallowed nervously.

"Certainly. This disease you have rots your bones and turns you into a mockery of the perfect German male. This condition of yours is a slap in the face to your Aryan ancestors. Surely you must see that."

To Kolger's shocked expression, the doctor returned another

empty grin. "You'll feel a slight pinch."

Kolger did feel a slight pinch as the doctor eased the needle into his upper arm. And then he felt the "steroid" as it left the syringe and coursed through the inside of first his arm then into his chest, where it settled like a sleeping kitten. He yawned and the exhaustion washed over him.

"When will I be able to see my parents?" Kolger asked, slurring his words.

"Soon," the doctor promised, as Kolger's eyes closed finally and forever.

The boy's head soon rested on his frail chest. The doctor reached out and took hold of Kolger's wrist, almost as if he were grabbing a side of beef. After a moment, he turned to the clerk behind the desk.

"Time of death: 9:15."

* * * * * *

Two weeks later, Gregor and Maria Fruskins received a telegram, informing them, regrettably, that their son, Kolger, had succumbed to pneumonia while in the doctor's care. The Reich Committee for the Scientific Registering of Serious Hereditary and Congenital Illnesses expressed its sincerest regrets to the grieving couple.

CHAPTER FOUR

Viktor ran his eyes over the small room once more to make certain he wasn't leaving anything behind. He certainly wouldn't be sad to see this little gem go. The bed smelled not only like old man, but almost as if an old man had died on it. The bathroom was streaked with yellowing tobacco stains and the carpet was crusty in several places. All in all, his room at the White Stag was not up to the level of any of his previous apartments. Hopefully, the room at the castle would prove to be more sufficient.

His two bags, he traveled light, were packed and stationed at the door. Doctor Obermayer had stated that someone would be at the White Stag precisely at seven p.m. to convey him and his belongings up to the castle and when Obermayer stated a directive, one could be assured it would be carried to the letter.

The discussion he had with his brother was knocking on the door of his mind again. He knew he shouldn't give it any more weight than it already had, but he was concerned...slightly. He hadn't been completely honest with his brother about the intent of the T4 program.

The program had begun with a stage of forced sterilizations on the patients. According to the reasoning, if they could halt the genetic and debilitating diseases from spreading to offspring, then maybe the purification of the Germanic race could be hastened. Of course, Viktor knew that the program had to spread from there. The Reich leaders would never content themselves with the simple prevention of debilitating diseases, at least not while current carriers were still around.

But August couldn't see the big picture. He never could see the big picture, even as a child. He only saw the immediate. He was narrow-minded that way.

There was an accident when Viktor was ten and August nine. The two boys and their friends, Rudolf and Nicholas, had been playing soldiers behind Rudolf's house while their parents worked.

With the Great War just over, there was no shortage of weapons available. Viktor had brought his father's army-provisioned rifle and August had their father's Mauser. Nicholas' father didn't have a weapon as he wasn't in the Great War and had to content himself with one of Rudolf's weapons, a rusty Smith and Wesson that Rudolf's father had picked up from a dead British soldier. Rudolf, of

24

course, had the group's favorite, a Parabellum MG14 machine gun.

The boys had spent most of the morning teamed-up, Viktor and August had to be on separate teams, and playing as Germany or Britain. Viktor and Rudolf were Germany first and soon had the British, August and Nicholas, captured and locked up in Rudolf's mother's fruit cellar. The younger boys complained that they were smaller than the other boys and it wasn't fair, so Rudolf and Nicholas switched sides.

Due to the constant insistence of their father, Viktor and August had always handled weapons with the safety's on, even when they had the weapons out of the house like they were told never to do and were playing with them without the expressed consent of their father.

Viktor had been teamed with Nicholas and felt sorry for the younger boy. He complained so much about using the rusty pistol that it almost drove Viktor crazy. Finally, Viktor had relented and allowed Nicholas to carry his father's Gewehr rifle while he took the handgun. They switched back for the next war.

As soon as this war started, they swooped around to where the other boys had been hiding, in the rear of the garden, which was probably unimaginative August's pick and reached a position directly behind the enemy. From where he stood, behind the towering grape vines that covered a wooden arch, Viktor could just make out his brother who was hiding behind a tomato plant and gesturing to his left where Rudolf probably stood.

Viktor saw August shake his head, point at his chest then point toward the barn where Viktor and Nicholas had their base. Apparently in agreement, August and Rudolf stood and made ready to storm the barn. At that moment, Viktor winked at the hidden Nicholas and both boys stepped out to capture their enemies.

Viktor realized much later that he had made two mistakes that day. The first mistake was not checking the chamber of the Gewehr that morning and the second mistake was not telling the younger boy to keep the safety on when he had the rifle. The younger boy must have flipped the safety off when he had the rifle. As Nicholas stepped up behind August and shouted "bang", Viktor stepped behind Rudolf and pulled the trigger of the rifle. With the safety turned to the off position, the hidden round in the rifle fired and tore a hole through Rudolf's left shoulder, dropping the boy to the ground.

Viktor froze; staring at the rifle like it was a snake, while Rudolf lay on his stomach alternating between screams and groans.

Viktor realized much later that the accidental shot had probably propelled him into his future career as a doctor. He had seen the blood, so much blood, and had felt so helpless. He had always been diligent to correct his own errors; his father had instilled in him that responsibility as the oldest of the Gottlieb brothers. If August broke something while Viktor was supposed to be watching him, Viktor got punished, even though they were only years apart. If a room wasn't cleaned, Viktor met the punishment. Heaven knows why his father had felt he needed that much more responsibility that his brother.

Before Viktor or any of the others could take action, Herr Berns, who lived next door had come outside, alerted by the shot, and was entering the garden. August was sitting on the ground crying and was obviously no help to anyone. Viktor was in a likewise condition, finally depositing the rifle on the ground and whispered, "I'm sorry" over and over. As Herr Berns approached, Viktor stood to take blame for the situation.

"We were playing and the rifle went off…"

Herr Berns, smelling strongly of alcohol, pushed Viktor roughly to the side. "Shut up, boy. Now tell me what happened here and don't smart off to me! I know your father and don't think he won't hear about it before the day's through."

Viktor spouted off a hasty explanation as Berns bent down to inspect Rudolf, who mercifully had passed out. Herr Berns grunted and stood up.

"You boys are in for one heck of a beating for this one. No mistake." He approached Viktor. "So, you the one that shot this boy?"

Viktor, still trembling slightly, nodded his head.

"It's a good thing you're such a green shot or you might have blown his head off." Herr Berns bent down and picked up the rifle. "Gewehr's got a mighty kick to it. Probably saved that boy's life."

Herr Berns leaned forward and patted Viktor on the head. "Now, don't worry about your friend. I've seen much worse. He'll live." He moved back toward his house. "Now, you boys keep an eye on your friend and I'll call the doctor."

They didn't have to wait long. The doctor lived two streets over from Rudolf's house and had Rudolf in his bed and patched up before his parents' arrived home.

Herr Berns was right on one account as Viktor and August's father, upon hearing about the incident, gave them both severe whippings. Viktor, being the oldest, got the harder of the beating.

To make his point, Viktor's father, after administering the punishment, had shoved the rifle in Viktor's face. "Don't you ever forget what this is, Viktor. It's not a toy. It's a machine used for killing. Don't ever pick up one of these again unless you're prepared to kill someone. Respect the weapon cause it certainly won't respect you."

And Viktor had cried after that. He remembered that point distinctly. He had cried most of the night and his stupid little brother had asked him again and again why he was still crying and Viktor didn't really know.

Luckily, Rudolf had survived to play another day.

* * * * * *

A man who introduced himself as Captain Oster arrived precisely at seven o'clock to escort Viktor to the castle. Never smiling and hardly helpful, the captain graciously held doors open as Viktor lugged his bags from the upstairs room down through the bar and out into the chill night air.

Once the bags were firmly in the trunk and they had been seated, Oster started the car and spoke for the first and last time during their trek up to the Castle.

"Doctor Gottlieb, I am in charge of security at Castle Zarfuyls. If there is any threat, real or perceived, it is my duty to meet and overcome that threat. Do I make myself clear?"

"Certainly."

Captain Oster placed the car in "drive" and moved away from the White Stag Inn.

He continued, "Due to the sensitive nature of the T4 program, it is imperative that all of my orders, to my guards or to the staff, are obeyed and carried out to their strictest fulfillment as quickly as possible. Currently, we are housing close to five hundred mental patients at Castle Zarfuyls, many of which are extremely unstable and dangerous. Never forget their potential for violence."

"I assure you, Captain Oster, that I have dealt with these type of patients before. I have plenty of experience…"

"Have you ever seen what you thought was a tame dog suddenly turn on its master? Animals, I've often thought, can sense dangers

27

that we humans are simply ignorant of. When it feels its life is threatened, an animal will take whatever precautions it must in order to survive. Survival of the fittest is not just for animals, doctor. Humans can be the cruelest of all animals. We've perfected our egotism."

"You're quite a philosopher, Captain Oster."

From there, they rode the rest of the way in silence.

* * * * * *

Once at the castle, and after asking a considerable amount of directions, Viktor finally found his room. To his satisfaction, the accommodations were slightly better than the room at the White Stag. Unfortunately, he was sharing a room with two other doctors.

A few minutes after he had finished unpacking and setting up his meager belongings, an orderly came to escort him to the Director's office.

Viktor was amazed at the intricate passages he passed on his way to meet the Director. He knew that he'd never be able to find his way around without the assistance of a guide, but the orderly insisted that he'd get used to it soon enough, even though most of the passageways looked similar.

As they entered a passage that in no way differed from the one they had just left, a door opened in front of them and a nurse exited. Viktor had only time to glimpse her facial features once before she passed them by and disappeared through a side passage, but one glimpse was enough to print an image of her permanently inside his thoughts. Whoever she was, he would make sure to see her again.

The orderly continued on, oblivious, and stopped at the door that the nurse had just left. The plaque on the door announced the office of Herr Obermayer, Director of Operations.

Once inside, the orderly withdrew, leaving Viktor alone with the Director, who inhabited the chair behind his desk like a long-dead Germanic king.

Herr Obermayer smiled with a slightly strained expression. "I apologize that I can't give you the full briefing, Doctor Gottlieb, but we are expecting another bus load of patients within the hour. Please be seated."

Viktor seated himself in the plush, leather armchair in front of the desk and waited.

"I will be mercilessly to the point." Obermayer continued. "You know why you're here and you certainly understand the extent of the

T4 Program and what the Reich hopes to obtain through that program."

Obermayer rose to his impressive bulk and stepped away from the desk.

"I also realize that you were appointed by none other than the Führer's Director of Science and Medicine to this post while the remainder of the doctors were hand-picked by myself. Don't let your appointment go to your head, doctor. You will be treated as your position demands, nothing less and certainly nothing more.

"Tomorrow, you will be given your instructions, but tonight," Obermayer glanced at his watch, "I'll need you in the courtyard with the rest of the doctors to greet the new patients. It's not something that is needed but a personal touch we give to make the patients feel more comfortable. Don't want to raise the anxiety level of them any more than we have to, eh?"

Obermayer smiled and sat on the edge of his desk. "Now, don't worry about the patients, Doctor Gottlieb. Captain Oster assures me of the safety of the staff. Simply do the job appointed to you and all will go quite smoothly here for all.

"You have about fifteen minutes before you're needed in the courtyard. As I said, we're expecting another arrival of patients and I enjoy introducing myself and the available staff as soon as possible. It helps them to understand exactly who is in charge here. The orderly should be waiting just outside the door to guide you back to your room. Please get on a clean, white uniform and I shall see you downstairs shortly."

Dismissed, Viktor exited the room. Obermayer's eyes narrowed slightly as he watched the young doctor leave.

CHAPTER FIVE

The Reich had converted the great hall in the castle into a dining facility. Gone was the dust, tapestries and memories of a bygone age and in their place were now forty-seven long dining tables, three serving areas, a full kitchen with two double broilers and, at the far end, on the dais, rested the three tables reserved exclusively for the doctors, nurses and residing guests of state. One such dignitary was Herr Drammels, recently sent from the head of the Reich Committee for the Scientific Registering of Serious Hereditary and Congenital Illnesses.

Herr Drammels slopped another copious amount of maple syrup onto his breakfast biscuits, took a massive bite and continued his diatribe, much to the chagrin of those around him.

"It all comes down to racial cleansing, he said to me while I held onto his hand. If the Germanic peoples can cleanse themselves of these foreign antibodies which have managed to invade our culture for the last forty years, if we can manage to isolate the shear godhood of the Aryan, we have a chance. Of course, I knew immediately what the Führer was referring to. After all, I had read Mein Kampf several times. One of the new classics, you know.

"But this," he waved his fork in the general area of those gathered in their gray jumpers on the lower end of the hall, "this is nothing but another manifestation of that hereditary impurity. Yes, it started with the Jews, and what doesn't? But who knows how far and how deep the infection runs. It's up to the doctors of the Fatherland to meet this disease head on. It is only through their valiant efforts that we will regain our rightful place."

Viktor surveyed Herr Drammels from around his upraised glass of orange juice. This man was a fool, like so many others now in positions of authority. How long would they have to endure his posturing and ramblings? There was honest work to be done.

Herr Obermayer gestured toward the outside world. "So, they haven't forgot about us in Berlin?"

"On the contrary," answered Drammels, "you are all very much in the Führer's thoughts. He talks of this program constantly, in between laments over the rocket program that is."

Obermayer leaned forward, snatching the lure like a hungry catfish. "Oh, are things not going so well for the rocket program?"

Drammels lay one forefinger against the side of his nose. "Let's just say that I have it on good confidence that we will not be seeing any new advances in the following few months."

Viktor promptly lost interest in the conversation, if his interest had ever been there. He took the brief respite to scan the crowd below for any familiar faces. But they came and went so fast that he hardly noticed.

Viktor had to admit that he was far from bored, but he was also far from challenged. As the most junior of physicians, he was left with the most plebian of tasks, only slightly higher than a nurse or orderly. For the first few weeks, he checked the patients in their separate rooms and observed the questioning process. After four hours of observing, he was required to write a summary paper, chronicling the summations of the more senior physicians.

The next few days saw him assisting the examiners with their procedures. They spent hours examining the brain tissue of the corpses, in hopes of finding some pattern, some regularity to the hereditary conditions. But so far, they had discovered no variant, no anomaly.

And then, he was rudely drawn from his musings by the raised voice of Herr Drammels. "I mean just look at them," he gestured toward the patients with a biscuit-laden fork, syrup dripping on the table, "they don't have any reason to be suckling off the Fatherland's teat, depriving the real heroes of Germany the care and attention they deserve. They are vermin and justifiably so."

"Here, here," uttered Robert Schessmacht, another of the junior doctors who was seated farther down the table.

"At least they're not as utterly repulsive as the Jew," cut in Obermayer quickly. "Although, not by much."

Herr Drammels considered this thought. "I'm not so certain. At least with the Jew it is an outside contagion, a rat that has wandered into the house. But with these…"he gestured again to the patients milling around, "these abominations, you have something else entirely. Imagine, gentlemen, if we had created something perfect and then, as we sat back to bask in the glory of our creation, we noticed an imperfection set by an enemy. These imperfections are the antithesis of the perfect Aryan, a mockery of what God Himself put perfect here on earth."

Down between the tables, a female patient with Down's syndrome slipped to the floor, upending a full tray of food and causing Drammels to spray food out of his mouth as he laughed

31

hysterically. The patient gained her footing and turned to a table full of patients, who were laughing. Without warning, the patient with Down's syndrome whacked one of the other patients in the head with her tray and soon the immediate area was chaos.

Drammels turned to Obermayer. "And there is my proof. They're less than animals. They're undeserving of this castle, this air, this gift of life. Surely, the Führer has dubbed them correctly as *Lebensunwertem Lebens*, 'Life unworthy of life'. Their infirmities have completely bereft them of their basic humanity."

Viktor took the moment of silence in between Drammel's bites and sermons to interject, "And how long will you grace us with your presence, Herr Drammels?"

Obermayer scowled.

Drammels, however, shoved another bite into his endless gape and continued, "Oh, I mustn't keep the Führer waiting. He directs me to make a complete report on all the facilities by this weekend. I'll leave Castle Zarfuyls at four this afternoon and head straight toward Schloss Hartheim."

* * * * * *

Martin peered cautiously up at the doctors seated at the dais. He didn't dare let his eyes linger overlong. They had all learned the lesson of young Skylar Finnel.

Shortly after arriving around a week ago, Skylar Finnel, a young German Swede, with a penchant for stealing and lying, paused, with a tray full of food and stared at the staff seated on the dais for what seemed like a full minute. Within a short stretch, Obermayer had motioned an orderly over to move Skylar along. After a few choice words with no response, the orderly had struck Skylar with a closed fist to the back of the head, knocking the boy to the floor. A few moments later and the boy was still on the floor, but his face was lying in a pool of drool as his arms and legs thrust out in a frenzy of epileptic activity. He had to be carried away and the other residents had heard nothing more concerning him again.

Martin took a few steps, before turning back abruptly. He had noticed immediately that Dieter wasn't with him. The great moon calf was still in line. He still struggled to find his way around the workings of the castle.

Martin reached out and grabbed hold of Dieter's elbow. "Come along, little moon calf," he hissed. "Mustn't keep the Führer waiting, shall we?"

32

He guided the blind boy to a table farthest away from the dais, where they sat among strangers. Within days of arriving at the castle, they had lost track of Louisa. The Spanish girl had simply disappeared. They had seen Helt once or twice, but the boy was staying in a separate room in a different wing of the castle and ate at a different shift. No, it was just Martin and Moon, alone again.

As Dieter wolfed down his breakfast, seemingly with relish, Martin picked at his and wondered, probably for the fiftieth time, if he'd ever get out of this castle. Oh, there were rumors floating around certainly. Martin had heard his share. The men in charge were getting rid of them.

And there were plenty of clues to validate the rumors as well. "Remember Gustaf, the kid with the breathing problem? Well, they took him into a room for questioning and we never saw him again." Or "Remember Marie? Yeah, that girl with the big lump on the back of her neck. Well, she just wouldn't stop crying in the middle of the night and they took her away and the next day, they came and got all of her things too."

Yes, there wasn't any shortage when it came to rumors. At the very least, the nurses and orderlies at the old sanitarium were cruel, but you could almost count on them to not kill you if you upset them. These new staff...well, you just didn't know. You put one toe in the wrong place and not only would you be in fear of losing the toe, but the foot and body as well. Best to keep quiet for now.

But sometimes quiet wasn't in the cards for Martin. Sometimes Martin felt an urge to yell an assault to the heavens. Sometimes Martin felt like he needed to argue with the men that hid in the walls. It was just so hard to think now after they took away his medications. He hadn't received one pill since arriving and that was another thing that worried him.

A few days ago, he had stood before a group of three older doctors, who asked him about a hundred questions, poked and prodded him and taken about a gallon of his blood. He was summarily dismissed and told that he would be seeing them again in a few days.

But it had almost happened. Right after the doctor with the white, crazy hair had asked him if anyone in his family had ever heard voices, and that was a story long in the telling, one of the men in the wall had come out and started talking derisively about Martin's mother.

Martin knew that no one else could see the men in the wall. He had known for quite some time, but that didn't stop Martin from seeing them, or having to listen to them. And often, maybe too often, Martin would rise to their baiting and argue right back with them. He knew they weren't real, or at least he knew he was supposed to believe that they weren't real. His parents had told him they weren't real and the doctors had agreed, and Martin, to some degree understood and acknowledged that fact. But simple facts didn't make the men go away. They were much too stubborn for that.

Luckily, Martin had ignored their threats and cajoling long enough to get out of the room. Of course, later, when he was alone, he let the men in the wall feel the full brunt of his wrath…but only when no one was around.

No, it didn't pay to be crazy in this place. There were too many unknowns.

He was nudged out of his reverie by Dieter's elbow. Glancing up, Martin noticed that the fat, suited man, the stranger, was slowly raising his girth from the seat. The other doctors rose as well.

* * * * * *

"And now, gentlemen," said Herr Drammels, "let us inspect your fine establishment."

The doctors rose with Drammels, as he broke from the table and headed down the dais.

When Viktor attempted to follow along with the little group, or follow a little ways until he could safely get away, he was halted by a firm grip on his shoulder. Turning, he was confronted by Herr Obermayer.

"A word please, Herr Gottlieb."

Viktor raised one quizzical eyebrow and followed Obermayer as he left the dais and took an alternate corridor. He was stopped as soon as they had gone from earshot of the makeshift cafeteria.

"I don't know what you think you're doing," said Obermayer, "but you will find your place, young doctor Gottlieb. When we have visiting officials sent straight from the Führer himself, only I will have direct conversation with them, unless they initiate the conversation themselves. Do I make myself absolutely clear?"

Viktor narrowed his eyes just slightly. "Yes, Director. You make yourself clear. I apologize for over-stepping my boundaries."

Obermayer waved the apology away. "No matter. Doctor

34

Hartford is sick in bed. He won't be getting out today, but I need his observations completed. I realize that you've never completed observations, but it really is simple. Inside observation room seven there is a clipboard. Attached to the clipboard are several papers with similar questions. You have twenty-five patients to meet with today. They will show up at the observation room. You won't need to get them. Simply fill out one paper each and place them in the drop box in my office when you are finished. Do you have any questions?"

"No, Herr Director," said Viktor.

"Good." Obermayer looked around the corridor, "Now, I will have to catch up with Herr Drammels and make sure that his visit runs smoothly."

With a slight smile and a wink, Obermayer clapped Viktor on the shoulder, turned and strode toward the cafeteria.

"Over-stepping your bounds quite a bit, aren't you, young Gottlieb?" Robert Schessmacht, the other young intern, stepped into the hallway recently vacated by Obermayer. "You've got some guts, Gottlieb, I'll give you that. The way you attempted to get in good with Drammels. They ought to give you a medal."

Viktor's face broke into a grin. The day after arriving at the castle, Viktor found that one of his roommates was this other young intern, from a small town west of Berlin. Schessmacht had kept Viktor up until three in the morning his second night, entertaining him with endless jokes about the French.

"Oh, and you didn't try to get in close to Drammels at all, did you Robert?"

"Here, here," answered Robert and both men laughed.

* * * * * *

It was around the thirteenth observation when a thought rose, uncontrollably into his mind. Why would a doctor need to do this?

Standing in front of the desk in his underwear was a small, practically emaciated boy named, Viktor had to look down at the paper to remember, named Reimund Hartmann.

The questions Viktor asked the patients covered the gamut from typical health and habit-related questions to queries about the patients' lineage. There were fifty questions in all. Question eight was particularly intriguing: Was your mother ever raped?

He had just finished up with Reimund. "You can start getting your clothes on as I ask these last few questions."

35

Reimund nodded nervously and began to get dressed as Viktor continued.

"Do you have any history of syphilis, gonorrhea, or any other sexually-related disease in your family?"

"No sir," said Reimund.

"And finally, at what age did you say your first word?"

"I don't remember, sir," said Reimund as he pulled his pants over his slight hips.

"Don't remember at all? Very well."

Viktor rang the buzzer on his desk and the door opened swiftly to reveal Stefan, the bull-shaped orderly. Stefan, without stating a word, herded Reimund out the door.

Turning around, Viktor took advantage of the slight break in schedule to place his tin coffee cup on the small burner located in the back of the room. As he re-heated his coffee, he heard the door open and close behind him. Without a word, Stefan led the next patient in and parked him before the desk.

"Take off all your clothes but your underwear and place them on the floor behind the chair please." Viktor stated, as he added more sugar to his coffee.

Slowly, Viktor eased his lips onto the rim of the cup and sipped. Ah, just the right temperature and consistency. He turned around and stopped.

There before him was one of the largest boys he had ever seen, with a sloping forehead and a shock of oiled black hair. The body was nowhere from being in fit physical condition, the stomach had long ago lost the battle with obesity, but Viktor figured that it would be no problem whatsoever for that patient to easily lift the large oak desk that stood between them. The patient had to be nearly sixteen or seventeen years of age, but his almost hairless torso belied any indication of puberty's onset.

The feature, however, that drew Viktor's immediate attention was the two pits where the eyes should have been.

"Name?" Viktor asked as he picked up the clipboard.

"Dieter Himmelbach."

CHAPTER SIX

Viktor shivered despite himself. It was cold in this part of the castle, although the patient in front of him didn't seem to be experiencing any problems. Maybe he had been raised in a colder climate. One could never tell. Even though the patients here were from central Germany, that did not mean they had been born and raised in central Germany.

There was something unnerving about those black chasms where the patient's eyes should have been. It was unnatural. They made Dieter Himmelbach seem a touch alien, something that did not belong among the human race. With a slight nervous twinge, Viktor shuffled the papers and cleared his throat.

"It states that you have been a resident of Brunsgord Sanitarium for just over five years. Is that correct?"

"Yes, sir."

"Yes, good," Viktor said. "And you are fifteen years of age?"

"Yes, sir."

Viktor glanced up to see Dieter staring directly at him. "And, um, you have been blind since birth."

Dieter smiled so slightly it was hard to see a definite change. "Yes, sir."

"I see."

Viktor, slightly unnerved at the sightless holes boring into him, reached for his cup of coffee, and only succeeded in knocking it over and losing his pencil in the process.

"Oh, that's wonderful, just wonderful." The doctor's eyes searched the room for something to wipe up the mess. He eventually noticed a cloth tossed idly on a nearby table.

As he passed Dieter on his way to the cloth, Viktor muttered, "You may as well sit."

Dieter obediently sat on the metal chair in front of the desk. After the towel had been retrieved and the mess blotted, Viktor once again attempted to complete the interview process. He grabbed the clipboard containing the questions and couldn't locate his pencil.

"I, um," he stuttered as he searched the desk and surrounding floor for his pencil, "hold on one moment."

Dieter allowed the young doctor to struggle for a moment longer before he spoke. "Your pencil is in the wastepaper basket beside your desk."

Viktor frowned, then turned to look down at the trash can. And there, below some wadded up papers was his pencil. He smiled and turned to Dieter.

"How did you know that my pencil fell in the wastepaper basket?"

Dieter smiled. "I have acute hearing. I guess it's God's way of making up for the blindness. When you spilled your coffee, you knocked your pencil into the waste paper basket."

"Hmm," said Viktor. "Thank you."

"You're welcome."

"Okay," said Viktor as he straightened his clipboard. "And tell me, does blindness run in your family or was there a more physical explanation for your affliction?"

"Well," considered Dieter, "as far I know blindness doesn't run in my family. Neither my sister nor brother was born blind like myself. Unfortunately, I was sent to the Sanitarium long before I could ask my mother any questions about my family history. But, doctor, if I could, can I get your name?"

"I don't think that's appropriate," Viktor answered. "Now, Dieter, do you have any schooling?"

"No, sir."

"And have you ever learned Braille?"

"No, sir."

"Do you have any Jewish ancestry?"

"Not that I know of, sir. Sir, why is that relevant?"

Viktor paused and smiled, just a tad bit cruelly. "It's a standard question to be asked every German citizen, Dieter. The Führer wants to determine if International Jewry is a cause of some of our societal ills. Now, let's…"

"And, is it, sir?"

"Is what, Dieter?"

"Are the Jews a cause of our societal ills?"

Viktor considered. "Our government and the majority of intelligent men in our country seem to believe so. Who am I to contradict their collective intelligence?"

"But what about Einstein and Freud, sir?"

"And how does a blind fifteen-year-old mental patient know anything about Albert Einstein and Sigmund Freud?"

"Well, sir," said Dieter, "like I stated before, I have acute hearing. There's rarely a conversation that doesn't go by that I can't pick up on. Doctor Bram, my previous counselor, was talking to another staff member one time about Einstein. He said that he didn't understand how a man as intelligent as Albert Einstein, with his ideas concerning relativity, could possibly be dismissed because of his Jewish ancestry. He said that maybe the government had gotten it wrong, at least in the case of Albert Einstein."

"It sounds to me like your Doctor Bram didn't trust the sensibilities of his leadership," Viktor said. "It also sounds like your Doctor Bram might not be holding a position as doctor for much longer with an opinion like that. Besides, Dieter, it's not polite to eavesdrop on other's conversations."

"Yes, sir. But, sir…"

Viktor held up a hand, even though Dieter couldn't possibly see it. "Please, Dieter, allow me to ask the questions."

"Yes, sir."

* * * * * *

Sometime between question 39 and 45, Viktor had come up with a plan to use Dieter. Of course, the word "use" did not enter Viktor's mind; it was more of a plan to allow the hulking blind boy to be useful.

There was a nurse. Of course, there was always a nurse. But this one had caught Viktor's attention on his first day at the castle. She wasn't a striking beauty by any stretch of the word, but there was something about her tiny nose, the shape of her face, something about the way she pursed her lips when completing an inventory that completely enraptured the young doctor.

There were other nurses at the Castle as well, but none that captivated his attention as clearly as this one. Within a few days time, Viktor had learned that her name was Olivia Kluge and that she hailed from Dusseldorf. She had worked at East Stutgard as well for a time, so maybe they had a little common ground to plant a decent conversation.

And, as the weeks had strolled past, he had attempted on more than one occasion to start some sort of conversation with her, but so far, all his efforts had resulted in less than nothing. In fact, more often than not, he had walked up on Nurse Olivia and one of the other nurses, giggling uncontrollably, which ended immediately upon sight of the young doctor.

He knew they were laughing at his expense but he didn't know why.

As they were wrapped up the initial questions, Viktor allowed Dieter to get dressed.

"So, just a few more questions and we're all finished, Dieter." Viktor placed the clipboard down on the table. "A while ago you mentioned Albert Einstein and his theory of relativity. How much do you actually know or understand about relativity?"

Dieter paused while sticking his head through his shirt. "Is this an official question, sir?"

"No, Dieter, it's a personal question."

"Yes, sir. Well, when you say the theory of relativity, are you referring to the special or general theory of relativity?"

"I, uh, I don't really know."

"Well, there are two theories of relativity. The special theory of relativity relates to physics in general. Basically it states that the laws of physics work the same no matter what state a person is in. If a person is standing still or moving at half the speed of light, the laws of physics will affect every person the same."

"And the general theory?" Viktor prompted.

"Well that one's kind of concerned with gravity."

"Gravity? But I thought Newton…"

"Yes, but there were some problems with the Newtonian theory of gravity." Dieter stated, fully dressed now. "Anyway, the Einstein theory was a lot different. See, in that theory, gravity is a result of the curvature of space-time."

"Look, Dieter, I'll be honest. Some of what you're talking about is simply foreign to me. I've read just a little on Einstein. I know about 'E' equals 'MC' squared, but that's about where it ends. When you start talking about the curvature of space-time, it's a little easy to get lost."

"No, doctor, it's really…" Dieter stopped and reached for the wet cloth that remained on the desk. "It's probably easier if I showed you. See, space-time, and you could probably just as easily call it space, acts like this cloth. When you place an object on the cloth, the cloth bends down because of the weight of the object placed on the cloth. If I placed another lighter object near the first object, the second object would tend to move toward the first object, right?"

Viktor nodded. "Because of the shape of the cloth, acting like a funnel."

"That's right. Just like a funnel. Anyway, that was how Einstein explained gravity. Gravity is really the funnel effect. It's the weight of one object affecting the structure of space-time, which correspondingly affects other objects."

Dieter paused for a moment and cocked his head, almost like a dog. "Not that I necessarily believe that theory of gravity. See, I can understand the curvature of space-time because it fits with how some other things work. But gravity, it's a little too much like magnetism. There's an attraction between two objects. Also, Earth has a north and south pole as well, just like a giant magnet."

Viktor laughed. "But then we'd all have to be made of metal, wouldn't we, in order for gravity to be magnetism?"

"Not necessarily. See, magnetism works on a sub-atomic level. It's not simply a magnet attracting a piece of metal. Its particles attracting like particles or particles repelling opposites. So, it's entirely possible that the earth and all other planets are giant magnets and we're attracted to the earth because it's attracting like particles in us. It would work the same with rocks, trees, whatever."

Shaking his head, Viktor reached down and grabbed the clipboard. "You lost me about three statements back. I don't understand how a young man with no education can be so well versed in physics."

"Actually, sir, that's an easy question to answer. Doctor Bram had a very special hobby that he enjoyed discussing with a certain other doctor at the Sanitarium."

"Physics?"

"Yes, sir. And, well, I just happened to be around and listening when these discussions took place and I picked up on a bit of the details."

"Still," said Viktor, "it would be a little like listening to two men speak a foreign language after a while, wouldn't it? I mean, physics, like any other pursuit, has its own technical language."

"Yes, sir, I guess it does. I guess, after a while of listening, you pick up the context of a word or phrase based on how it's being used. So, I guess you're right. It is a little like learning a foreign language. But God seems to have gifted me with the ability to pick up on certain languages faster than others might. When you spend all your focus on listening, it's amazing what you can understand."

Viktor looked down at the clipboard. "Yes. I suppose so. Dieter, it's been a pleasure talking with you. I can't say I understood everything we discussed, but I definitely enjoyed the conversation."

"Thank you, sir."

"Viktor."

"Excuse me, sir?" Dieter asked.

"My name is Viktor."

"Yes, sir. I know sir. I heard another doctor use your name a few days ago while I was mopping the main hall." Dieter smiled sheepishly. "Sorry. Eavesdropping again, I'm afraid."

Viktor smiled as well. "We'll have to break you of that nasty habit some day, won't we?

"I suppose we will sir."

Viktor stood suddenly. "Well, that's it for today, Dieter. We'll see you again in a few days."

"Yes, sir."

Dieter moved toward the door, opened it and left. Stefan, the orderly stationed outside the door stuck his head in as soon as Dieter had disappeared down the hallway.

"Doctor Gottlieb? Shall I send in the next patient?"

Viktor stared at the opposite wall, lost in thought. "Give me about ten minutes, please."

CHAPTER SEVEN

One of the numerous drawbacks to being so low on the seniority list was that Viktor often got picked for the most menial of tasks, especially if the rest of the staff were needed elsewhere. As it happened, one of the patients, a young, doe-eyed girl with Romanian ancestry who possessed an unhealthy attraction to fire had been playing with a book of matches in a mop closet. Unfortunately for her, one of the mops had been recently used to clean up after a diesel spill and the whole closet, including the majority of the patient's hair had been devoured by the resulting conflagration.

So, the downside was that instead of interviewing patients, Viktor was forced to spend the entire afternoon hauling patient's bodies from a chamber in the basement of the castle to the furnace room, as the usual workers were busy taking care of the fire and the resulting clean up. The upside was that the other two interns were assisting him along with one of the guards.

Viktor returned to the chamber just as the guard and Konrad Werner, an extremely sour, young doctor who wore a perpetual look of disgust, were hauling another body out.

"This is disgusting work. They should make the patients do this." Konrad grumbled as he hefted the body. "I mean, you don't know what sort of lice or other vermin has been wandering over this body. We could all catch the plague."

"Maybe you'll find a pet," said Robert, rounding the corner.

"Grow up, Schessmacht." Konrad said as he and the guard left.

After the other two had left, Robert bent down to one of the bodies and plucked off a handkerchief, which he wrapped around his head like an old lady.

"Is it true, Viktor?" Robert asked. "Am I immature?"

"Well, that's one word for what you are," Viktor said as he glanced woefully around the room. There were still maybe twenty bodies left to move.

"You know, an old crone once told me that different people use different tactics to handle the stress of extraordinary situations."

Viktor glanced up at the handkerchief on Robert's head. "And is that how you handle the stress? By placing disease-infected clothing on your head?"

Robert swiped the rag off his head and threw it on top of the nearest body. "Okay, maybe you're right. I'm sure there are healthier

43

ways of dealing with the situations around us. But my pa always said that a good laugh is a whole lot healthier than a morning walk, cause you can get run over by a truck if you're out wandering around. I'd like to see a truck run me down in here."

Viktor looked toward the door, half expecting Konrad and the guard to return at any moment, even though the entire round trip took about thirty minutes for each body. "Come on, we better get going."

"What are you? Afraid of Konrad?"

"Hardly," Viktor answered, as he bent down to lift a nearby corpse by the armpits. "But I'm not ashamed to say that I think that guard is a little too loyal to the cause for my tastes."

Robert bent down to pick up the feet. "I know what you mean. I have a feeling that the minute he sees one of us not sweating our last drop for the glory of the Fatherland, he'll report us to Captain Oster and who knows where that lunatic will send us."

They began to move the body out of the room and down the corridor.

"You better watch how loudly you express your opinions, Robert. Certain statements always have a habit of reaching around to bite you on the backside sometime in the future."

"And where did you hear that nugget of wisdom?" Robert asked, grunting between words. "No, but you're point is well taken. The Reich has ears everywhere. I had a friend who I worked with as an intern. Fine fellow but a little too expressive of his opinion when he should have guarded his tongue a little closer. For whatever reason, he lashed out one night on a tirade against the Führer and I could have sworn that it was just the two of us working that shift. Somehow, though, someone found out. Not two days later, in the deepest, darkest hour of the night, a pair of Gestapo turned up at the hospital and dragged him away, never to be seen again."

"Is that a true story?" Viktor asked.

"Do you doubt my veracity, good surah?"

Konrad and the guard appeared suddenly in the corridor, temporarily squelching the conversation.

"So, I knew it would take you forever to fetch another one." Konrad said as he passed them. "You're going to make us do all the work because of your laziness."

"Laziness?" Robert asked. "Why, you do us a disservice. We had to pick just the right one. Not any corpse would do you know."

"Meaning that you had to find the lightest one," Konrad called over his shoulder as he disappeared down the hall.

Robert paused to make sure that Konrad and the guard were completely gone. "Okay, hold up for a moment," he said as he dropped the feet of the corpse to the ground.

"What's the matter?" Viktor asked. "Getting a little heavy for you?"

In answer, Robert reached into his front shirt pocket and removed a pack of cigarettes. He plopped one into his mouth. "No, it's just my break time."

"Funny," remarked Viktor.

Flourishing a match from another pocket, Robert lit his cigarette and took a deep puff. "Ah, now that makes it all worthwhile."

Viktor glanced nervously around. "Are you sure you want to be doing that here, Robert? You know Obermayer has strict rules about smoking in certain parts of the castle."

Robert bent down and hefted the legs of the corpse. "How is he going to see me here? Besides, you worry too much, Viktor."

"I've got good reason to worry," said Viktor. "There was this man I worked with back at East Stutgard, a capable surgeon, very capable in fact. He was regarded as one of the best cardiac surgeons in Berlin. Of course, his Achilles heel was that he was a complete drunk. You never could tell if he would show in the operating room sober or barely able to stand on his two feet. His condition was covered up for a while, primarily because he was well connected. Unfortunately, his situation leaked out and the Gestapo got him one night. As far as I heard, they placed him in an internment camp. His wife raised such a complaint that they took her away as well. They're both probably still there, if they haven't died."

They reached the furnace room, which was boiling hot and manned by a short and swarthy looking man who ignored the two doctors as he continually fed shovelfuls of coal into the waiting maw of the furnace. After a moment, Viktor and Robert managed to dump the corpse on the table next to other bodies.

As the corpse hit the table, a note card fell from an interior pocket to the floor. Viktor automatically bent down and reached under the table to retrieve the paper.

Robert paused at the door, waiting for the other man. "What is it?"

Viktor turned the card around to reveal the name "Kolger

Fruskins" printed in neat script on the reverse side. "Patient identification card."

He placed the card back under the patient's frock and left.

* * * * * *

In a few hours, their work completed, the doctors stood outside the furnace room, far enough from the door so that they didn't have to endure the heat. The guard had excused himself rather abruptly as soon as the last corpse was delivered and the man who worked the furnace closed the door as soon as he was able.

Konrad Werner was the next to break ranks. "Well, gentlemen, there's a book in our room with my name on it. She calls to me."

"Better not keep her waiting," said Robert as Konrad took off. "It's probably the only woman he'll ever get into our room. Well, Viktor, it's just you and me now. Want to have some fun?"

Viktor yawned. "I don't know. I could really use a shower. I smell like death."

Robert sniffed in exaggeration. "Yes, you're certainly no flower in bloom, young Gottlieb. But don't think about showering just yet. Your day of sweating has just begun."

"I think I'll pass," answered Viktor.

"Come on," said Robert. "It'll be loads of fun. You could use some relaxation after a hard day of transporting corpses."

"Yes, but relaxation that involves sweating? I think I've had enough…"

"Bah," Robert said as he threw a friendly arm over Viktor's shoulders and propelled him down the corridor. "This is a good kind of sweat."

* * * * * *

A half hour later found the doctors outside the back wall of the castle. Robert had to make a quick stop back at their room to get a golf club.

"So, this is your art of relaxation, eh doctor?" Viktor remarked as lounged with his back against the castle wall and stared down the hill toward the river Gaart which circled the castle.

In response, Robert swung his five iron down and chipped another clod of dirt forty feet into the air and into the awaiting river. He smiled as he watched the dirt fly.

"Of course. Is there any other way for respectable doctors to relax?"

Robert loaded up another dirt clod. "So, tell me, young doctor Gottlieb, what do you think of all this business?"

"All of what business?" Viktor attempted to throw a clump of dirt from where he was sitting to the river below and managed to miss by at least twenty feet.

Robert swung again. "What we're accomplishing here with the T4 Program. Are these miserable handicaps really such a stain on the future of the Reich? How important is our research on them? Are we just now delving into the future of the Germanic race as a whole? Please. Please enlighten me as we are far beyond the eyes and ears of the secret police."

Viktor tossed another piece of dirt. "We're never out of the reach of the secret police." He frowned, "Oh, I don't know. Some of what we're doing here seems a bit excessive, I must admit. But where science is concerned, I think our work here has merit. Certainly. And think about the miserable handicaps as you call them. How much life do they actually have to look forward to? Are we doing any favors by keeping them alive in our asylums? Are we progressing where we can actually cure any of their behavioral problems or are we simply prolonging the inevitable?"

"You're quite the philosophical young doctor, Herr Gottlieb. I can't say that I've given the situation as much thought as you have. Why, you're as dedicated as a master theologian."

"You're thinking of my brother, there. Honestly, I hadn't given it much thought until recently. A patient was always a puzzle waiting to be solved. And that's where the elation came from, I believe. You work at the problem long enough, roll it around your head and then, suddenly the solution hits you. That's all this is to me as well: A problem waiting to find a solution. Will we ever find the cause of physical or mental retardation so we can stop it from appearing in future generations? I don't know. But if what we're doing here gets us one step closer to finding a cure, then, yes, I believe we're doing the right thing."

Robert held the club out to Viktor. "And now, Herr Doctor, I believe it's your turn to take some of your aggression out on these innocent dirt clods while I lounge about and philosophize about the meaning of our existence and the reality of our work."

Shrugging, Viktor rose and took the offered club, while Robert exchanged places, watching him swing a few practice times.

"Ah, see," said Robert, "I knew, as a doctor, that you had to have some limited experience with a golf club. It's part of our secret internship program."

"Actually, you're right," said Viktor as he chipped a chunk of dirt into the waiting river. "I picked up the game at the request of a couple of college classmates. Although, I must admit that I haven't picked up a club since college."

"It's like riding a bicycle or making love to a beautiful woman, eh, Herr doctor?" Robert said as gazed longingly at the passing clouds. "Some things just naturally get ingrained inside a man's head and never let go no matter how hard we try to shake them free. You know, as a child, my parents forced me to go to church every Sunday: rain or shine, sick or well. It didn't matter one bit either way. I had enough of the Mass crammed down my throat that when I was old enough, I promised myself that I would never, ever step foot inside a church again. And I never have."

Robert turned his head to find Viktor looking directly at him. "In fact, I turned completely the other way. I became a dedicated atheist at college and had a year or two where all I did was hound the Christians on campus, debunking everything they uttered. God, I was a terror. Ah, but it was all in good fun."

Robert flopped himself onto his stomach and stared out into the river. "You know what I couldn't stand about the church the most? It was the way they just waved every explanation away. They didn't have enough guts to admit that they didn't know. Why is the sky blue? Oh, it's a miracle of God. Why do we eat animals and they don't eat us? Oh, it's just the way God designed the world. And why? Why? Why? Oh, a little boy should just have faith. Have faith? That's just another way of saying we need to stay ignorant and trust the man in the sky. God has all the answers. You should just stop using your brain and start trusting in Him. What a load of rubbish!"

Viktor swung. "Seems like you have a problem with organized religion, Herr Schessmacht. Are you certain you didn't get beaten by the parish priest a little too much as a child?"

"Organized religion!" Robert arced a stone into the water far below. "The only thing they're organized about is keeping their people ignorant and blissfully unaware. They have absolutely no idea the damage they're doing to people."

"Sounds like we hit a raw nerve there, Herr Doctor," said Viktor. "Care to tell me about your childhood?"

"No thank you, Doctor Freud. If I'm going to be psychoanalyzed, I like to pay for it so I know I'm getting my money's worth. Who knows what I'll end up with you?"

"Suit yourself," said Viktor as he lined up another dirt clod. "So, I fail to see the connection between any of this and what we're doing here. Do you have a point good doctor, or just a lot of hot air?"

Robert rose to his feet and approached Viktor. "My point, doctor Gottlieb, before I was so rudely interrupted, was simply that even though I have fiercely attempted to smother my religious upbringing, it continues to return unbidden into my thoughts at every turn. Little phrases jump out at the oddest moments. Memories and verses from the Bible attack me while I attempt to concentrate. Images of saints appear in my dreams staring disapprovingly and wagging their fingers at me as I find myself clothed only in my underwear during the day of my college finals. In short, good doctor, I find myself haunted."

Viktor took a moment to look Robert over to attempt to perceive how much was simple bluster and how much was serious. "And have these images told you anything recently?"

"Yes," said Robert. "As we were moving those bodies earlier, a little voice in my head kept repeating, 'Thou shall not kill. Thou shall not kill.'"

"And is that really relevant in our situation here? Are we killing anyone? When Adolf Hitler himself calls these patients 'Life unworthy of life', can we really consider them any different? After all, how can we take away the life of something that didn't deserve it in the first place?"

Robert reached down and plucked the golf club from Viktor's hands. "I didn't say I believed the small voice. I just said I heard it."

CHAPTER EIGHT

The interview process would be a lot more enjoyable, Viktor thought, if it weren't for the patients. They were all so depressing. Every story was a tale of woe and abuse. Every scar had its own epic journey. And, add all that to the added delight that the majority of the patients had an almost Herculean time at attempting to pay attention and staying on track. Viktor felt, not for the first time, like a Kindergarten teacher.

"No, Martin. Let's get back to the original question," said Viktor slowly. "We were originally discussing the prospect of a history of mental illness in your family."

Martin answered in kind. "And I was explaining to you, Doctor, the story of my great Uncle Fritz who once fought an entire war naked."

"And I can certainly understand why you would want me to hear about your Uncle Fritz as his behavior is certainly indicative of some sort of mental illness. However, I was really referring to your more intimate family members."

Martin cocked his head. "Doctor Gottlieb, I don't know what you are referring to, but if this is some kind of hint toward sexual abuse or impropriety, I must protest that..."

Viktor closed his eyes and brought his hand up, gently rubbing his forehead. He could use more aspirin. "No, no, no. By intimate, I meant closer family: your mother, father, siblings. Did any of them have a history of mental illness; reveal any symptoms such as the ones you've been exhibiting?"

"I did have a brother who thought he was Napoleon."

Viktor's eyes clicked open as he brought his pen to the notepad. "Ah. Now tell me a little about this brother."

"I can't."

Viktor's eyes narrowed. "Why not?"

Martin's eyes dropped to his lap. "I just made him up."

Viktor brought the pencil down hard on the table. "Now look, Martin, we've been in this room for a very long time now. If you'd like, I can call in an orderly to assist us."

"And just how would he assist us?"

"He could make it very difficult for you if you don't tell the truth."

Martin raised his hand to his chin, rubbing it. "I see. And how would one, say hypothetically, make it extremely difficult for one such as I? Hmmm? Would he pull out my toenails one by one, doctor? Would he rub chicken fat all over my body? Do you think he would do that?"

Viktor rolled his eyes then brought his open hand down heavily on the bell at his desk. "Orderly!"

"Wait. Wait, doctor Gottlieb. I was just having a little fun."

The door opened and Stefan stuck his head in. "Yes, Doctor?"

Viktor raised his eyebrows questioningly at Martin.

Martin half-raised his arms in surrender, causing Viktor to smile slowly. "I was just checking to make sure you were out there. Can you get us a pitcher of water please?"

The orderly's eyes narrowed. "Of course, doctor? Will that be all?"

"For now," Viktor answered. Once Stefan closed the door, he continued. "Now, Martin, no more games. I have a job to do and you've got a job to get back to. Let's make this short and quick, shall we?"

"Of course, Doctor," said Martin.

Viktor folded his hands and laid them on his desk. "All right. So, let's talk a little about your immediate family history."

"Okay. Let's talk about that." Martin said as he leaned forward. "Let's talk about how I was raised by a drunk who beat me every night he was home, which wasn't once a week at best. Or suppose we talk about how I was raised by my Uncle, who locked me up in the house until he could ship me off to an institution the first chance he got. Or we could talk about how I was locked in a cage almost nightly, like a pet rabbit. Yes, they fed me when they remembered to, but they kept me naked just in case I had a bowel movement."

Viktor fought to not let his emotions show. "And your mother?"

"Oh, my mother, now that's a great little story. My father, in one of his more lucid moments was sitting in his favorite chair one night, a bottle of whiskey on the table beside him and I was probably seven or eight. I didn't even ask him about mother. I never did anything that I thought might get him mad at me, at least not intentionally. Sure, the men in the wall were there from day one, but I didn't listen..."

Viktor interrupted. "The men in the wall? Who are they?"

"The men in the wall? Did I say that? I don't know what I could have been thinking. Now, let's get back to the story, doctor. I won't

51

be lead astray by your active imagination."

Martin leaned a little further back in his chair. "Now there I was, just thanking God that he wasn't angry tonight. He had been back that time for three days and maybe he'd gotten tired of beating on me. Who knows? So, he was in a pretty peaceful mood, and he started talking about the days when he first met my mother. They had grown up in the same village. In fact, they had attended the same school until he had been forced to leave to help out the family.

"And then Da starts mumbling about how he was never good enough for her until she started to be a whore. I was pretty young, but I knew what a whore was. And so, instead of keeping my big mouth shut until he rambled on and hit unconsciousness, I asked him what he meant. He turned to me and he had this huge smile on his face, like he knew a secret that could hurt me worse than any punch ever could. And he tells me how my ma, straight out of school, had to work as a whore to support her family and how my da came to her one night and got her pregnant. Well, they were just going to get rid of me, but my mother got a little soft or something and out I came nine months later."

Martin folded his arms, but continued. "Not long after I was born, one of my mother's regulars got a little rough and strangled my ma. Of course, my grandmother was watching me at the time. But she wouldn't keep me. Da said she told him that she wouldn't keep me. So, there I was, living with my father, who had to work double shifts and who knows what else to support me and this bastard child he never wanted. No wonder he beat the hell out of me. I would have done the same in his place."

The door opened, admitting Stefan with a tray holding a pitcher of water and several cups. He left without a word. Martin gestured at the water.

"Do you mind if I get a drink, Doctor Gottlieb? Reminiscing is thirsty work."

Viktor nodded. "Certainly."

Martin calmly poured some water into one of the glass and sipped. Satisfied, he placed the half-full cup back on the tray.

"Thank you, Doctor Gottlieb. Now, the main question you were asking was about the mental state of my immediate family. Well, I think anyone would have to question the sanity of a drunk that nearly beat to death his only son or a woman who decided to become a prostitute, was practically encouraged to become a prostitute to support her mother and father. But I don't think anyone would classify those actions as belonging to the mentally unfit these days. They're practically common occurrence."

"So," started Viktor, "do you think you would have turned out any better if you had been raised by a loving father and mother?"

"Well, the way I see it is we can't live in a fantasy world, Doctor Gottlieb. We have to live with the life we've got, even if it's a god-awful mess."

* * * * * *

After the interviews of the day, Viktor retired to his room for, hopefully, some solace and a soothing hot shower. The staff quarters were the only place in the castle with reliable hot water. The rest of the castle fed off an old hot water heater that had seen much better days.

Viktor opened the door and immediately blew out a sigh of relief. The room was dark, meaning that Konrad was absent. The man seemed to spend every waking hour in the room. And even though he glided through his time by reading, a quiet pursuit by any measure, Viktor seemed to feel Konrad's eyes on him no matter where he was at in the room. It was like inhabiting a room with a ghostly painting: the eyes following you no matter where you traveled.

Viktor crossed the room in the dark and went directly toward the desk, flipping on the lamp in the process. He crossed over to his dresser, got a change of clothes from the top drawer and headed toward the door before halting.

Someone was in the room with him. Viktor looked over to the right to see Robert sitting on his made bed, his legs stiffly in front of him and his eyes staring out into dead space, as if he were still staring into a dark room.

"Robert?"

Robert took a moment before raising his eyes to meet Viktor's. What Viktor saw in those eyes immediately made him shiver.

"Viktor? You're back early, eh?"

Viktor stepped closer to his bed. "Robert, are you all right?"

"All right? Yes, I suppose." He shook his head, as if to clear it. "Just a rough day. I've been doing a bit of thinking."

Viktor tossed the clothes down on his own bed and sat down on it, facing the other doctor. "What's going on, Robert? You look as if you've just seen a ghost. Is it that inner voice again?"

53

This caused Robert to glance up sharply at Viktor. "Voice? I don't know. Maybe I'm just been over-worked. I feel terrible."

"Well, maybe you're coming down with whatever's taken out Doctor Hartford. There's plenty of room for sickness to fester in this old castle. That's all it is, Robert. You just need a bit of rest and relaxation. Say, maybe we can go into town sometime soon. Get away from this place."

Robert smiled, erasing years from his tired visage. "You're right, of course. I've just been working too hard and not getting enough sleep. So, young Gottlieb, your mental prowess has conquered another patient. You must have studied under Freud."

"That Jew?" Viktor raised his eyebrows. "I wouldn't be here if I had. The Reich would never elevate a known collaborator with someone of the Jewish persuasion. Why, it's tantamount to attempting to kill Hitler."

"It probably would kill Hitler if he knew any one of his precious handpicked few were collaborating with the Jewish menace."

Viktor stood and grabbed his clothes. "Well, it's good to see you back to your old self once more. What set you off?"

Robert's eyes glazed over. "There was this patient I had been interviewing: a pretty young girl. Well, she would have been pretty except for the split lip and the black eyes. Apparently one of the guards had been attempting to take advantage of her and she fought back. He didn't appreciate her resistance and he let her know about it in no uncertain terms."

"She got away easy, then," said Viktor. "Any patient found laying hands on a guard, even if the guard provoked it, is to be summarily executed. Patients aren't to touch any of the staff. You know that. That's classic first-day Obermayer."

"Yes, I'm well aware of the rules in the restrictive Castle Zarfuyls. Thank you ever so much, Doctor Gottlieb for your remedial lessons. I just…I don't know. I can't help coming back to what seems like a double standard in regards to how we treat the patients and how we treat each other."

Viktor sat back down on the bed. "This is becoming quite an issue with you. We'd better settle it before you decide to think some thoughts that wouldn't follow along the party lines."

"I think I'm so far outside of party lines, that I wouldn't recognize them if I crossed them."

"That may be, young doctor Schessmacht. But regardless of your political leanings, we've got to get your thinking back in line before you decide to do or think something rash."

Viktor glanced around the room, noticed the door open a crack and moved to shut it. Once it was firmly closed, Viktor moved to sit next to Robert.

"Look, I'm not saying that I'm an avid Nazi enthusiast either. I've had some definite issues and thoughts pop into my head that you could say were very unorthodox. But thinking that way now is not safe. We both know that. We've both heard stories of those who've challenged the party and ended up never being seen or heard from again. You told me one yourself. Keeping your head down and staying quiet, that's the way to go."

Robert looked up at Viktor with one tear rolling down his cheek. "I don't know how long I can keep up with this façade. Okay, it's easy to say that they're just vermin and their lives don't mater. And it even easier to say that what we're doing is furthering the cause of science and people way down the line from us will benefit from what we're doing now. But I just can't stop feeling like what we're doing is wrong."

"And what happened to the fellow a few days ago who said he heard a small voice but didn't believe a word of what it said?"

"It's getting louder every day. Look, Viktor, I'm not a religious man. I don't trust people who say they've heard from a higher power or that they're following this or that deity. They seem like complete idiots to me. This…this is something different. Maybe it's my conscience. Maybe it's the ghosts of my long dead, religious parents. I don't know. But the more I'm here, the more revolted I become."

"Think about it, Robert. What would you do? If you walk away, you may as well say that you're leaving the Nazi party. They'd never let you do that. If you try to fight what's happening here, if you take a stand against this place, they'd ship you off to one of the work camps. Just give it a little time. Maybe a solution will present itself."

"Yeah, of course you're right. Look, I don't know what's come over me. I haven't been feeling right for some time now. And, I agree. If I keep on this line of thinking, I'm just going to go off and do something stupid."

"Now you've got it, Robert. No need going off half-cocked. Look, there are no perfect situations. But we've got to make the best out of what we've got."

Robert grinned. "Very philosophical of you. And who was that from: Aristotle? Socrates? The Buddha perhaps?"

Viktor rose to his feet. "Actually, I heard it from one of the patients today. It sort of stuck with me."

Viktor placed one hand on Robert's shoulder. "We'll get through this fine, old man. You'll see."

The door opened and Konrad Werner, his nose in a book, wandered in. He stopped just inside the room and stared for a moment at Robert seated on the bed and Viktor standing above him with his hand on his shoulder.

"Hope I'm not interrupting something, boys."

Viktor smirked at Robert and grabbed his clothes up once more. "Oh, don't worry about us, Konrad. We were just discussing deep and very philosophical matters."

"Yeah," added Robert. "I'm almost certain you would not be interested."

"Hmm," Konrad stated as he seated himself on the chair by the desk. "I'm certain that your deep and very philosophical matters would be well beneath me."

"All right, gentlemen," said Viktor, "I'm off to scrub some of the stain of the day off me. Don't have any fun without me."

"Don't worry about that, Gottlieb," said Robert as the other doctor left.

As he walked down the hall, away from his room, Viktor could hear Robert starting in on Konrad.

"So, tell me, bookworm," said Robert, "would you even know a deep and philosophical matter if it came at you in a dark alley?"

CHAPTER NINE

It had been almost a week since his encounter with the blind patient. In that space of time, Viktor had accomplished well over thirty initial examinations. Whatever was keeping Doctor Hartford confined to his bed must have been a mighty germ indeed. No matter. Viktor welcomed this time, even though the endless ramblings and dislocated answers he received from some of the patients threatened madness on himself.

He just couldn't get the image of that hulking patient with great caverns for eyes out of his imagination. That blind boy with no schooling seemed more intelligent than any number of men the young doctor had known, and that included fellow doctors.

Viktor had attended a lecture one boring Saturday while as an intern. It was an impromptu lesson from the chief of staff from the mental facility wing during an otherwise meaningless day. Apparently the man had fancied himself a teacher and was attempting to impart his wisdom on the group of young interns. Regardless of the intent, the only substance that the young doctor had gleaned from the incident was that the man was an egotist, schizophrenia was not spelled with an "f", and that, according to a new report, idiot savantism was closely linked to autism.

Now, the subject of idiot savantism was extremely interesting to Viktor and, he remembered he sat still and attentive during that interlude especially. Apparently, there was a class of patients suffering from mild retardation where the social aspects of the patient were more retarded than the mental facilities. In fact, there was a class on the autism spectrum disorder that consisted of those who were extremely proficient in a single matter of expertise, say physics, and could converse at great length and intricacy on that topic. Dieter seemed to fit in this category nicely.

He had seen the blind patient a few times in the last few days. Once Viktor was aware of his presence, he saw Dieter almost everywhere. Of course, this wasn't the largest of castles by any account.

Viktor had a few hours of free time, a rare occurrence, when he decided to seek out the blind patient and determine for himself if his knowledge was limited to physics, as he had supposed. It was an hour after lunch, but Viktor didn't have the beginnings of a clue as to where the patients might be when they were not in examinations. He could just as surely be in his room as on a detail somewhere on the castle grounds.

The doctor started in the West wing, where the patients were housed but, after locating the dormitory, did not discover Dieter. After another fifteen minutes of hunting, the doctor finally located the blind patient mopping up the cafeteria along with several others.

Viktor approached him confidentially. "Dieter, if I may have a word with you."

Dieter looked around, slightly confused. "But, my mopping…"

Viktor, in answer, nodded once. He hurried over to the orderly that was currently overseeing that detail and, after a few words, walked back to Dieter.

"Come along," said Viktor. "Leave your mop. I have a few more questions for you."

Dieters dutifully left the mop by the bucket near the door, removed his apron and followed after the doctor. They moved in silence until reaching the doctor's study within minutes.

Each of the interns shared a study on the same hallway as the accomplished doctor's offices. It was rarely used and little more than a closet with bookshelves, but it served its purpose.

After closing the door and seating Dieter, Viktor moved to the bookshelf and removed a specific brown leather clad book, entitled *Thus Spake Zarathustra*. He thumbed through the work, until stopping at a particular chapter.

"Are you familiar with the works of Friedrich Nietzsche?" Viktor asked.

Dieter smirked. "Our government certainly seems to be."

"What do you mean?" Viktor said, a bit strictly.

Dieter dropped his sightless eyes, apologetically. "I'm sorry, if I overstepped my bounds. I am only aware of what I've heard said about Nietzsche, not what I've read."

"No, I apologize, of course you could never had read any of his work," said Viktor, quickly. "I didn't mean to sound disapproving. It's just in this day and age…"

"…It's best to make sure that you're not overheard denouncing the government," completed Dieter. "Yes, sir. I understand."

"So, what do you understand about our countryman and philosopher Nietzsche?"

"Only what I've heard, sir, only what I've heard."

Viktor replaced the book. "And what would you say about

Nietzsche's central conclusion that God is neither necessary nor alive in the world today?"

Dieter chose his words carefully. "I would say, sir, that for Nietzsche, God is most concretely dead. There are choices and conclusions that we make in this life that forever burn those bridges we strove so hard to construct. Nietzsche came to the conclusion that God is dead because that is where his strivings led him. How could God be alive in a society that evolved to a point where man is God?"

"And have we become such a society?"

"We've always been such a society, doctor. Man will constantly strive against anything that seeks to limit him, to place controls on him. We may have been created in God's image, as my dear mother told me, but every second after that we have striven to mold and shape ourselves into something hideous so as to escape His grasp. We struggle to bend ourselves into beings that no longer have to submit to God's authority."

"But wasn't Nietzsche right?" Viktor countered. "Didn't Darwin, after all, prove that creation is just a myth, a fable that is broken by the truth of evolution?"

"I've heard that word thrown around like it was the defense of many things, sir. Evolution has defeated God. Social evolution means that we don't have to live as the cavemen once did, ever reliant on the concepts of good and evil. But ultimately, sir, if evolution is correct, doesn't that simply make life meaningless?"

"Why should it?"

"If we all come from protoplasm and will end up reverting to protoplasm, then any choices we make in this life will affect no one and lead to nothing."

"Isn't that a pretty bleak assessment?" Viktor asked. "It sounds a bit extreme."

"Is it? I wonder if Nietzsche would say it is. After all, wasn't his apex, his Übermensch or superman, wasn't that the top of the evolutionary scale? Didn't Darwin just support everything that Nietzsche proposed in his philosophical discourses? Didn't Darwin support the superman ideal that Nietzsche so wistfully desired?"

Dieter stopped and smiled broadly, a wide, innocent smile. "Now, sir, is this what you wanted to see me about? Did you want to plumb the depths of my philosophical knowledge?"

Viktor sat down behind his desk. "No. I was curious about your intellect, to tell you the truth, Dieter. It seemed implausible that you could have no schooling but be so well versed on physics and, now, philosophy. Are you sure you don't want to change your story concerning your education?"

"Why would I change the truth, sir? No, as I stated before, when one of the senses is absent, it may be that the others compensate for the loss. I do a lot of listening and I have an extreme amount of time to contemplate and mentally digest."

A knock sounded at the door, jarring both the doctor and the patient.

"Yes," said Viktor, "who is it?"

"Doctor Gottlieb?" It was Obermayer.

"This discussion will have to wait until later," said Viktor. To Obermayer, he announced, "One moment, please," and rose to his feet.

Dieter also rose and was led by Viktor to the door. "I have one favor to ask you, so please exit and wait for me around the corner."

Dieter nodded and opened the door to the consternated face of Herr Obermayer. Obermayer lifted an eyebrow as Dieter excused himself out into the hallway. Dieter had no sooner closed the door than the director spouted at the young doctor.

"What is the meaning of this, Herr Gottlieb?" Obermayer practically shouted, barely controlling his confusion turned to rage. "How dare you have a patient into your personal study! You've read the rules very closely, I'm sure. There is to be absolutely no doctor-patient fraternization."

"Herr Obermayer…"

"Whatever you have to say cannot be excuse enough. I am seriously considering punishment for this infraction."

"You don't understand, sir. His case is unusual and I was simply studying the patient further."

This piqued his curiosity. "Unusual, you say? In what way?"

"The boy has been blind since birth and has received no schooling, but he understands the most intricate concepts, such as the theory of relativity and philosophy."

Obermayer snorted. "Relativity! That's just Jewish science, a pseudo-science. A monkey could understand that."

Viktor was not so quickly undermined. "Yes, sir. But nonetheless, I find it amazing that one who has no proper schooling could comprehend the theory of relativity, let alone understand the philosophy of Nietzsche."

"Nietzsche? But come, what is this really about, Herr Gottlieb? So a blind boy with no schooling can understand complex concepts? So what? How does that serve the Reich? Are you suggesting we contact the Führer and tell him that we have a candidate to assist in the development of his rocket program or that we have an invalid who may be a brilliant tactician?"

Obermayer, temporarily spent, sat down exhaustedly in Viktor's chair while the young doctor obediently took the chair on the outside of the desk.

"Now, forget whatever mad chase you're conducting" continued Obermayer, "and onto more pressing business. Unfortunately, Doctor Hartford's health has taken a turn for the worse and we were forced to take him to a nearby hospital last night. It is unknown how long it will be before he returns, if he returns."

"That's terrible," said Viktor. "Do they know what he has?"

"No," said Obermayer. "Unfortunately, the doctors at the hospital have no idea either, although they are running tests. So, I will need you to continue the initial interviews. Now, how many initial interviews were you able to complete within the last three days?"

Viktor's hand absently reached out toward the pile of papers on the corner of his desk. "Just over fifty, Herr Director."

Obermayer frowned. "Just fifty? No, you'll need to step up the pace immediately, Viktor. Before Herr Drammels proceeded to his next assignment, he confided in me the Führer's direct wishes in this project. The Führer expects great resistance within the Catholic-controlled areas to this program, of which Sterlingaart is definitely one. We must be processing over two hundred patients weekly or Herr Drammels will have no choice but to transport the patients to another, faster processing center, perhaps to one of the work camps."

"One of the work camps? But they're ill-equipped to properly handle this amount of patients."

"They'll manage. But let's make certain it doesn't get to that point. I enjoy my job here, Viktor and I would prefer not to get another, such as head medic at the Russian Front, if you get my meaning."

"Yes, sir. I do."

"Now, young Gottlieb," Obermayer reached into his pocket and removed a creased and folded paper. "About your request for

61

temporary leave on Saturday…"

Viktor looked down. "I guess this increase in productivity means that all leave has been canceled without further notice."

"Nonsense. I can't have my staff suffering from exhaustion. You need to get out and get some fresh air once in a while. It does you a world of good, believe me. So, quite the contrary. Your leave has been granted."

"Thank you, Herr Obermayer."

"Think nothing of it." Obermayer smiled crookedly. "So, tell me, what plans have you concocted for this weekend? Going for a little sightseeing in the town, perhaps check out the local nightlife? I remember what it was to be a young doctor in a new town. Of course, Sterlingaart hardly has a day life, never mind nightlife. But, you never know."

"Actually, Herr Director, as fate would have it, my brother lives in town. I thought I'd go and have lunch with him this Saturday. And maybe look to see what this fair city has to offer."

Obermayer laughed a large, hearty laugh and rose to his feet. "Well, don't get into trouble. If you get thrown into the local jail, don't expect me to come running along to get you out."

Viktor rose with him and followed the Director to the door. Obermayer placed his hand on the knob and turned once more to Viktor.

"And remember what I said earlier about fraternizing with the patients. I heard it from one of the orderlies that Doctor Hartford had been getting a little too friendly with several of the female patients. Who knows what sort of disease these people have?"

Obermayer laughed again, opened the door and proceeded down the hallway.

Viktor counted a full minute after the Director had left before leaving the study. He walked into the center of the hallway, looked both ways and then called out in a quiet but firm voice, "Dieter!"

After a moment, Dieter appeared around a corner and into the doctor's view. "I thought you had forgotten all about me."

Viktor grinned. "Maybe I should have. Come into my office. I have a favor to ask you."

Dieter waited until they were fully in the study with the door closed before responding. "Yes, sir. And does this favor involve mopping your study?"

Viktor crossed the room and sat behind his desk. "Dieter, I've thought about what you've said, about your acute hearing and was wondering if you could do me a slight favor. Now, it's just a bit embarrassing, so I would appreciate your confidence on this manner."

"Of course, sir. Anything."

Viktor paused before starting. "It's...There is a nurse named Olivia..."

He was interrupted by the sudden laughter of the blind patient, which inexplicably caused Viktor to seethe. "How dare you!"

Dieter sobered immediately. "No, sir. I apologize. It wasn't your request. It's just that there is a nurse...You see, sir, that I had told you that I get a little bored and I listen to conversations some times."

"You mean you eavesdrop."

"Yes, sir. Well, I happened to be listening to these two nurses one day and they were talking about this particular young doctor. Well, I'm sure you can imagine who they were referring to. And they stood there discussing this young doctor for quite some time and what they thought of him."

"And what did they think of the young doctor?" Viktor requested.

Dieter smiled faintly. "Well, that's the thing. They were wondering if the young doctor actually liked women."

"What?"

"Yes, sir. See, one of the nurses, named Olivia, thought that the doctor had started to show some interest in her, but had never followed up with an actual conversation. She was actually quite disappointed. So, you see, sir, when you brought up that name..."

"Yes, of course." Viktor paused, staring straight through Dieter into the wall behind him. "Well, it looks as if I don't actually have a favor to ask of you after all, Dieter. You answered my question."

"Then I'll go, shall I?"

Viktor looked up at the blind patient who stood by the door and smiled. "I'm sure we'll see each other soon."

* * * * * *

By the afternoon, Viktor had struck up a conversation with Olivia the nurse when he had conveniently crossed her path as she made her rounds from dormitory to dormitory. Within the course of the conversation, Viktor inquired as to her activity on Saturday. Was she free to meet him in Sterlingaart sometime after noon? And, of course, she was.

CHAPTER TEN

Viktor made one stop before retiring to his bedroom. Near the kitchen was a tiny room that held a public use telephone for staff only. And, of course, there was a slight line waiting to use the phone.

Half an hour later, after tactfully attempting to dodge several conversations, Viktor was alone in the room with the telephone. He stared at the phone for a moment before realizing, fruitlessly, that he didn't have a clue if his brother had a telephone in the parish house and, if he did, what that number might be.

He decided to call the one person who might know how to get in touch with August.

"Mother, this is Viktor."

"Oh, Viktor, it is so good to hear from you." As usual, his mother thought she had to yell over the phone. "How are you, my son? Keeping warm in the castle?"

"Yes, the castle is very warm. You don't have to worry about that at all. They take care of us very well up here. Look, ma, I'm looking for August's phone number. Does he have a phone at the parish?"

"Yes, of course. What good would a parish priest be without a telephone?"

After a few more minutes of convoluted communication, Viktor was able to wrestle the phone number from her but he had to promise her that he would come to church with her again on the next Sunday. That was just like her: always holding what he wanted for ransom until she could get what she wanted.

He called his brother next and quickly set up a time to meet him in Sterlingaart on Saturday. Considering how demanding his position could be, it was a wonder that he was able to have some time to himself.

After the calls, Viktor headed straight back to his room. The door opened, apparently startling Robert, who was doing something on the desk. Quickly, Robert turned around, effectively blocking whatever was the on the desk.

"Viktor? Back so soon? I thought you'd be in interviews all day long."

Viktor eyed him suspiciously, but wandered over to his bed. "They certainly felt like they lasted all day. Had a run in with Obermayer over a patient though. That was…enlightening."

"I'll bet. Everything's been quiet here." Robert had moved in concert with Viktor, so the desk's contents remained hidden. "So, going to take a shower, I shouldn't guess?"

"What are you up to, Robert?" Viktor stepped closer to the other doctor.

"Nothing. Nothing at all. Why do you ask?" Robert's voice certainly seemed nonchalant, but he had begun to sweat.

Viktor could just make out a pitcher and glasses on the desk, along with some sort of bottle. "Having some sort of celebration are you, Robert? What are you doing?"

"Look, I'll tell you what I'm doing, but you have to promise me you'll stay out of it." He stepped away from the table, revealing a pitcher, three glasses and a bottle of champagne. Hidden just to the side of the bottle was a small prescription vial.

Viktor bent forward and picked it up the vial. "Chloral Hydrate. Knock out drops?"

"Look, I can't take it anymore. I haven't had a decent night of sleep since I got here. It's Werner's incessant snoring. It's driving me insane."

Viktor placed the vial back on the table. "Okay, the medicine I can understand, but why the ruse? Why do you have champagne, a pitcher and glasses?"

Robert sat on the edge of his bed. "The chloral hydrate isn't for me. It's for Konrad. Look, I can't stand his boring, cultured voice droning on and on about inconsequential issues any longer. I just wanted to shut him up and have a night of peace. I was going to mix it with the champagne and propose a little celebration."

"What are we celebrating?"

"I don't know. I haven't got that far. Anniversary of us being here for three weeks."

Robert dropped his head into his hands. "I'm cracking up. Admit it."

Viktor picked up the vial and placed it in his pocket before moving to sit on his own bed. "I don't know what to say, Robert. I'm no psychologist. Perhaps this place is getting to you. Maybe you should go talk to Obermayer."

Robert raised his head to look directly into Viktor's eyes. "Oh, yes, that makes perfect sense. What do you think they would do with me, Viktor? Do you think they'd prescribe a weekend in a Swiss resort village to calm my jangled nerves? Or maybe they'd just discharge me and send me back to my mother and father. We're sorry, but your son just couldn't take it anymore. We're afraid that the mental illness wiped off a little on him."

"I'm pretty sure that you can't catch crazy, Robert."

"I wouldn't be so sure about that one, Viktor. If everyone else is talking about the elf in the corner, sooner or later you're going to start wondering if maybe you don't see it because there's something wrong with you. And then maybe you'll just start seeing the elf too one day, not because he's there or ever been there but because everyone's got you convinced that he should be there."

"Robert, I'm convinced of one thing: you need rest. And I don't think drugging Konrad is the answer to your problems. Although it is tempting to consider. If talking to Obermayer isn't the answer, then maybe you should just get sick for a little while. You're a doctor. Start assigning yourself some symptoms and lay low for a while until you feel a little bit adequate. You should be able to fake a fever and, if need be, I can substantiate any story that you want."

"You know, Nietzsche took chloral hydrate regularly until it drove him insane," said Robert, with a distant, airy quality to his voice.

Viktor abruptly stood up, marched over to Robert and grabbed him by the shoulders. Violently, he shook the doctor for several moments before Robert reached up, grabbing his arms.

"Stop," said Robert. "I'm all right."

Keeping hands on the other man's shoulders, Viktor lowered his head until he could look directly into Robert's eyes. "I don't think you are all right, Robert. I think there's something going on in that head of yours that wants to break loose. I think that once you're out of here, that you're going to be due a nice, long vacation just to get back to a semblance of order. But I think for now, as your personal physician, you just need to get some sleep. I would prescribe you something, but in this case, I don't believe that would be in your best interest. Drink some champagne."

Robert's eyes, once they met Viktor's were once again lucid. "Look, you're right. I'll get some rest, maybe say I'm sick come Monday if I'm still off. Thanks for helping me out, Viktor."

Viktor stood. "Just get some rest, Robert. Put that champagne to some good use."

As Viktor turned and headed toward the door, Robert got to his feet. "I'll follow your instructions to the letter, my physician."

* * * * * *

66

The medications were kept in a locked cabinet in Dr. Obermayer's office, which prompted Viktor to wonder how Robert would have been able to secret it out in the first place. He wouldn't have any fear of running into the Director at this hour, as Herr Obermayer was more than likely retired in his own suite. The more immediate question, however, was how Viktor would return the vial to its proper place within a locked cabinet that rested in an equally locked closet.

Luckily, Viktor encountered no one through the hallways on his way to Obermayer's office. He had an excuse ready, looking for Herr Obermayer, just in case, but that proved unnecessary. He reached the office, turned the knob and slipped inside. Getting into the office was the easy part. Obermayer never kept his office locked. There was no need. Anything of value was either resting inside the locked closet or stayed with him in his own suite. Besides, if there were an emergency and someone needed a pharmaceutical at an odd hour, it hardly made sense to wake up the Director just to get into the cabinet. The night doctor had keys as well.

And one of the night crew, a certain older doctor who had looked kindly on Viktor since the day he had arrived at the castle, had lent him the key under the pretext that the young doctor was performing some late night duties on a direct order from Herr Obermayer himself. Viktor indulged in the tiny lie, knowing that he would be in and out of the cabinet and have the keys back in the older doctor's hands before anyone was wiser.

The office, of course, was deserted and dark. Viktor, recalling the general layout of the office, moved cautiously across the floor and toward the giant oak desk. Once to the desk, he felt around the top until he located the lamp, which he switched on, flooding the room in soft light.

Viktor's eyes checked out every dark recess in the room before convincing himself he was alone and moving toward the closet. There were actually two keys on the key chain and the larger one fit the lock on the closet door. He stepped inside the enclosed space, feeling rather than seeing the door start to slowly swing shut behind him. Quickly, he reached up and pulled on a string that turned on the light in the closet before the door shut completely and encased him in darkness.

The cabinet itself was standard issue and was kept in the order of most hospitals. It took Viktor moments to locate the precise shelf and return the Chloral Hydrate. Seconds later and the cabinet was locked up tight. Viktor smiled to himself as he opened the door with his right hand and pulled the string, killing the light with his left.

He shut the closet door behind him and started toward the desk before his eyes followed quickly by his body froze. A pair of man's boots rested lightly on the table's surface. The boots belonged to the man sitting in the chair behind the desk.

"Herr Gottlieb, how interesting." Captain Oster said. "Do you know that I regularly make rounds down this particular hallway at least five times nightly? Well, you can imagine my chagrin when I noted the light was turned on. After all, the doctors on the night shift rarely need medications or anything else as they are amply supplied. So I thought to myself, who would possibly be in Herr Obermayer's office at this hour."

Viktor straightened himself in a manner that he hoped would be intimidating. "Captain Oster, I appreciate your diligence, but I can assure you that I'm here only on official business. You see, Doctor Herzog…"

Captain Oster waved his hand dismissingly. "Yes, I'm well aware of who Doctor Herzog is and I'm also well aware that he would not send you up here to get medicine for any purpose as you hold no spot whatsoever on the night shift."

"How dare you," said Viktor. "What are you implying: that I'm breaking in to steal medications?"

Oster shook his head and removed his boots from the table. "Oh, I wouldn't dare do that, doctor. Besides, the keys are still hanging from your hand, so you obviously didn't break in."

Viktor clenched the keys in his hand subconsciously.

Oster continued. "And that's why I've come to several possible conclusions. Either I have a doctor with a possible addiction problem on my hands, I have a doctor who is a thief, or I have a doctor who is a thief for someone else. Now, you know as well as I do the Reich's attitude toward those poor fools who don't have enough will power to stay away from powerful substances. Addiction is simply not tolerated, doctor. It is seen as a sign of weakness. What would happen to a doctor that is found to be abusing substances? He would be shipped off to a special prison immediately."

Oster rose to his feet. "The Reich has a similar attitude toward those who cannot control their sticky fingers. This is a time of war, doctor, and those in leadership simply do not have the time nor patience to coddle those who have problems. A thief in some countries would have his hands removed at the wrists. Can we in war time expect any less?"

Oster made his way slowly around the side of the desk toward Viktor. "And we've made our way around to the final suspicion. Perhaps you were stealing an item for someone else. Maybe you have a doctor or a staff acquaintance, who desperately needed medication. Maybe they were hiding some secret that needed to be kept quiet. Maybe if that secret got out, it could potentially ruin that staff member. So, they sent you in their place."

"You have an incredible sense of imagination, Captain Oster," Viktor said. "The truth is much more simple than all the maybes you could fashion."

Oster sat on the desk. "Oh, then enlighten me, Doctor Gottlieb. I'm dying to know why a young doctor, who should be in bed at this hour, has borrowed a key from another staff member and made his way into a locked medications cabinet."

"The medication was for me. I've been having some troubles sleeping. One of my roommates has a problem with snoring and I haven't had a good night's sleep in some time. I borrowed the keys from Doctor Herzog so I could get a couple of pills to help me sleep tonight."

Oster smiled. "Ah, that's it then."

Viktor turned to go. "Yes, now if you'll excuse me..."

Oster held up a finger. "Oh, Doctor Gottlieb, one last thing. You see, I'm a suspicious man, always have been. That's probably why I'm the Captain of the guard. Been a problem since I was very young. Anyway, may I see the pills you removed from the cabinet?"

Viktor hesitated, thinking swiftly. "Ah, you see, that would be a problem because I wasn't removing the pills, I was replacing them. I had got them earlier and was just now putting them back."

Oster smiled, never taking his eyes off of Viktor's face. "It's funny how a story can change over time. Almost as if it had a life of its own."

"So you think I'm lying to you, Captain? I can assure you that my roommate, Doctor Shessmacht can back up my story. If you'd like we can go down to my room right now and discuss it with him."

"That won't be necessary, doctor. I'm sure Doctor Shessmacht would verify any story you told."

Oster walked toward Viktor until their faces were scant inches apart. "Doctor Gottlieb, like I stated, I'm a very suspicious man. And once my suspicions have been raised, it's very hard for me to put them to rest once again. I don't know exactly what is going on tonight and, honestly, as long as you're not jeopardizing this project, I don't much care. But I can guarantee you that if I feel that you're a liability, if I feel that you're participating in some activity that could be hazardous to anyone here, I will not hesitate to lock you up immediately. Do I make myself clear?"

"Of course, Captain Oster."

"Good night, Doctor Gottlieb. Pleasant dreams."

Viktor moved away from Oster, who smelled faintly of alcohol, and toward the door. Resting his hand on the knob, Viktor turned to see that Oster had once again sat on the edge of the desk and was eyeing him still.

"Good night, Captain Oster," Viktor said.

Oster grunted and nodded his head.

* * * * * *

Once Viktor got back to his room, he found Robert peacefully asleep and in a snoring contest with Warner, who was half in and half out of his own covers. His foot knocked into the champagne bottle that lay at the foot of Robert's bed.

Viktor glanced down at the other doctor, who looked completely different, not so haunted, when he was asleep. He knew, deep in his heart, that he should convince Robert to talk with one of the senior doctors as soon as possible. Something was going on with him that couldn't possibly bode well.

CHAPTER ELEVEN

The men in the wall were driving Martin absolutely nuts. They never let up anymore. They didn't let him sleep, get any rest, do anything. They popped out and started picking fights when he was on the toilet. It was too much and, without his medication, it soon became beyond anything he could endure.

He had been through several more interviews after the initial one and he had just barely been able to control his outbursts. He knew he was close to slipping up though. He'd felt himself almost letting go in front of that younger doctor...Gottlieb. God, he was so tired. He couldn't go on like this forever with ragged nerves and a frayed mind.

Martin thought Dieter may have sensed his moods, as the great moon calf was quieter than usual. He probably had thoughts running through his mind as well, although you wouldn't know it from looking at him. Hell, maybe he had men in the walls who drove him crazy too. You never could tell with that big mooncalf.

Dieter was one of the reasons that Martin had attempted to control himself for so long. He knew that if anything happened to him then the mooncalf would be lost, completely alone and defenseless. But it was getting to the point where Martin could really care less about keeping track of the aimless blind boy. He had his own problems to worry about.

By now, he and the remainder of the patients knew beyond any doubt that the rumors of patients being exterminated if they didn't fit some unknown criteria were real. He saw the smoke coming from the smokestacks day and night. He had seen, along with several other boys, the clumps of hair mixed with ashes that rained down from the smoke-lined skies.

It didn't take a mathematician to realize that when you saw busloads of patients entering and none leaving that they had to be going somewhere. He glanced around at a cafeteria that seemed to contain just about the same number of patients that were here when they first arrived.

Dieter was behind him in line, as usual, and moving with absolutely no motivation whatsoever. The mooncalf must have sensed the hopelessness all around him as well. This must have been what a cow felt like when it was guided into a slaughterhouse.

The orderly working the food line didn't bother to ask him what he wanted for breakfast. Instead, he just slopped a stinking mound of mush onto his tray and motioned Martin on. As the pile hit his tray, one of the men in the walls decided to pop out.

"Well, lookee there," said the man who had popped out from the wall directly behind the serving orderly. "Mush for the mush-head. If only you had come out of your mama looking a bit more like that mush, then maybe you wouldn't have been abandoned as a wee baby. Maybe if you'd have been a bit more mushy, you could have made your old ma proud and not made your dada run away like he did."

Martin could only stare, vacant-eyed at the man half in and half out of the wall.

"But that's probably what you wanted, wasn't it?" The man in the wall continued. "You probably wanted your old ma all to yourself, didn't you, Oedipus? Wanted to take your old man's place once and for all."

Martin narrowed his eyes and whispered, "Shut your face."

The serving orderly motioned with his chin. "Get a move on, boy."

Martin dropped his eyes, obediently and continued along the line. After a moment, he heard Dieter's furtive whisper at his side.

"Martin, are you okay?"

"Yeah." He couldn't raise enough strength to be cruel to the blind boy.

In a moment, as he was reaching for an offered glass of orange juice, the other man who lived in the wall popped his ugly head out.

"Well, lookee there, folks. Martin's got himself a nice, cool glass of freshly squeezed orange juice." The man in the wall mocked. "What a fine, refreshing drink that would be. Made by an orange squeezed delicately but firmly between his old ma's thighs. Oh, how poetic."

"You shut up," he said just a little loudly.

The orderly looked down at the boy with alarm turning into anger. "What did you say to me, boy?"

Dieter moved up quickly and gently pushed Martin along. "He didn't say anything, sir. He's just tired. Must still be asleep."

"Just get moving," said the orderly.

Dieter nodded quickly and rushed forward until he bumped into Martin again.

"Stop it," slurred Martin.

72

Dieter grabbed the other boy's arm. "Come on, Martin, we've got to get to a table, eat and get out of here."

Martin shrugged off Dieter's hand. "Get your hand off me, mooncalf!"

Dieter whispered furtively, noticing that Martin now had the attention of several orderlies. "If you don't calm down now, they're gonna take you away. You've got to get a hold of yourself."

Martin considered the advice for a second before nodding and shuffling toward the nearest table. They sat for a moment in silence before Dieter realized that he was the only one at the table who was eating. He couldn't even hear Martin's strained breathing.

"Martin?"

But Martin had never sat down at the table. With a glazed look in his eye, the boy continued to stare at the wall beside the entrance door, where one of the men in the wall had emerged and was currently hurling abuse at him.

"And that's something else, isn't it?" The man in the wall stated. "You think that man you lived with was your daddy? You never have met your father. Your father wasn't a man after all. Your father was a stray dog. Your mother got crazy drunk one night, drifted out into the woods and met a dog. Nine months later and out slopped Martin, eager to douse the world in flames, eh?"

Suddenly Martin hurled his tray at the wall just as a doctor was entering the cafeteria, effectively splattering the doctor, the wall, and a nearby table with mush.

"Shut your fat face," roared Martin. "I'm tired of you! Day and night, you go on and on about my mom and dad and you won't let up."

"Ooh, what are you gonna do about it, Martin?" the man in the wall teased. "Gonna come beat me up? Gonna tell your fat, old whore of a mother on me?"

Martin screamed in primal rage and ran at the wall, beating it with his hands, until blood flowed down his arms.

An orderly, who had been drawn by the screaming, jumped at Martin, knocking him to the ground. Martin, however, grabbed for the nearby tray and used it to repeatedly whack the orderly.

"Get away from me!" Martin screamed as he hit the orderly. "You're with them, aren't you? Then you'll get it, just like they will!"

Viktor, the doctor who had been entering the cafeteria just as Martin's dam had burst, quickly leapt onto Martin's body and tried to restrain his arms. Martin thrashed with the tray and managed to strike the doctor's temple with it, knocking Viktor away.

By that time, another two orderlies had run up and were trying to pull the first wounded orderly away while attempting to get under the arc of the swinging tray.

"Get away from me, all of you!" Martin screamed. "I've had enough of all of this and I'll kill the next one of you apes that comes close to me."

One of the orderlies who had almost placed one hand on the wounded orderly's ankle was struck suddenly in the temple with the tray, knocking him to the ground.

"How does that feel?" Martin yelled. "Wanna come get some more?"

Viktor had momentarily regained his senses after a moment of blackness had threatened. As Martin's tray wove a deadly wave toward the two orderlies crouched in front, Viktor rushed from behind and pinned Martin's arms to his side. The tray fell noisily to the ground.

"Martin, listen to me," shouted Viktor. "It's Doctor Gottlieb. You have to calm down."

Martin bucked and screamed as the two orderlies approached him. One of the orderlies, with blood dripping down the side of his head where the tray had struck, suddenly lashed out with his foot and kicked Martin in the stomach. Viktor could feel and hear the air escaping from him.

As the same orderly pulled his foot back for another blow, Viktor spoke up. "Look. Let's just get him out of here and restrain him somewhere instead of trying to use him as a football."

The orderly nodded. "Yes, sir. Sorry, sir."

Viktor rolled his eyes. "Just help me get him to a nearby room."

As they dragged the boy from the cafeteria, Obermayer, who had been sitting at the table on the dais, approached and walked with the small party.

"Viktor, I saw the whole thing," Obermayer said, slightly out of breath. "Are you all right?"

"I think so," said Viktor. "But that orderly may need some medical assistance. Where do we take the boy?"

"I'll see to that orderly. Take the boy into observation room five."

Obermayer hurried away to offer what medical services were

needed to the orderly as Viktor and another orderly named Laubert hauled the suddenly still body of Martin out of the cafeteria and into one of the adjoining rooms.

As soon as they had entered and closed the door behind them, Martin, who had only been feigning unconscious, ripped his arm from Viktor's grasp and jumped at the orderly. He landed on Laubert's upper body and knocked both of them into a nearby wall and onto the floor.

As Martin struck the orderly repeatedly about the head and chest with his fists, Viktor looked around the room anxiously for any sort of medication that might subdue the patient, but the only vials in evidence were the ones used by the teams to administer lethal injection to the patients. Finding nothing, not even a chair he could use to knock the patient unconscious, Viktor once again entered the fray.

As Viktor attempted to restrain the young patient while simultaneously trying to not get hit with a flailing fist, the door crashed open behind him. Obermayer strode in just as Viktor managed to restrain Martin's arms.

"Let me go," screamed Martin, as he thrashed against the doctor.

Viktor looked pleadingly up at Obermayer, who was doing something on the table against the wall.

"Sir," said Viktor, "Can you give me a hand?"

The orderly was moaning on the floor directly in front of them.

"Just a moment," Obermayer called over his shoulder.

One of Martin's hands broke free but was quickly restrained again. The boy screamed loudly, which echoed through the room.

Obermayer turned around with a loaded syringe in his hands. "Please hold him tightly, Viktor."

The young doctor recognized the syringe and what was inside. "But, sir, that's…"

Obermayer interrupted as he moved toward the pair. "It's just a sedative, Doctor Gottlieb. I just want to calm the patient down a bit."

Martin's eyes grew larger as he focused on the needle approaching him.

"Now, now, son." Obermayer cooed to the patient. "I just want to calm you down for a moment so we can all think a little more rationally."

"But, sir…" Viktor began.

"Just hold him steady," Obermayer said gently as he inserted the needle into the patient's upper arm.

As soon as the formula was injected, the patient's entire body threw itself rigid, almost knocking off Viktor's grip. But the young doctor held firm as he slowly felt the body begin to relax. After a moment, the body became completely limp.

Viktor released the body to the ground and looked to the orderly, who was still moaning. As the doctor assessed Laubert's condition, Obermayer stuck his head out of the room and called for a couple more orderlies.

"You didn't have to kill him, sir," Viktor said as he checked the orderly's slight head gash. "I had him restrained."

Obermayer looked at the young doctor with a slightly cocked head. "What's the point, Viktor? I just saved us a little time is all. We would have had to do it eventually."

"Yes, Herr Director," Viktor said as he rose to his feet.

Two other orderlies entered the room and looked around.

"I need one of you to get that man to the infirmary immediately," said Obermayer, pointing to the fallen Laubert. "I need the other man to take that patient to the examination rooms by the crematorium."

As the two orderlies moved to complete their separate missions, Viktor took the opportunity to rest against the table. Obermayer companionably walked up and rested a hand on the young doctor's shoulder.

"So, how was the orderly?" Obermayer asked.

"Oh, he'll be fine," replied Viktor, slightly distracted. "Just slight head trauma, but he should recover quickly."

Obermayer smiled. "Well, that's good, then. Isn't it?"

"Yes, sir."

Obermayer looked the young doctor over quickly. "Any bruises yourself?"

"No, sir."

"Then you better go get yourself cleaned up as well. Don't you have a day in Sterlingaart ahead of you, young Doctor Gottlieb?"

Viktor sighed. "Yes, Herr Director. I suppose I do."

Obermayer laughed and laid his arm on Viktor's shoulders, guiding him out of the room. "A day away from this place will do you some good, Viktor...especially after what you've just been through."

76

＊ ＊ ＊ ＊ ＊ ＊

Viktor had to wait over an hour before he could catch a ride into Sterlingaart. He could have walked, but one of the orderlies who often made trips into town told him that it was an extremely difficult trek and, besides, the cook's assistant went every Saturday and why not catch a ride with him?

So Viktor found himself riding in the passenger seat of a beat up truck with an apparent lack of shocks, next to a heavy, balding motor mouth of an assistant cook.

"You know, I feel really walled in up at the castle at times and I just gotta get out and see the countryside, breathe the fresh air. Not that the scenery is half bad in Sterlingaart either. There's a few pretty frauleins walking the streets. They haven't all left to join as nurses. You know what I mean?"

The question shook Viktor out of his daydream. "Excuse me?"

"I asked if you knew what I meant?"

"About what?"

"Ah, never mind, doctor." The cook's assistant waved the thought away. "I can tell we're on two different planes. See, I'm here with the world, and you're wherever doctors go when they're not working on people."

Viktor was on a completely different plane. He was back in that examination room watching a young man who obviously needed real help receive a needle full of death instead.

He became a doctor so he could save and protect human lives. Sure, they were conducting research on the patients, trying to locate and partition the part of the brain that may have led to some of these conditions. If they could gain any insight into these conditions, maybe more wouldn't have to suffer, maybe more children could be born without these debilitating infirmities. And wasn't that what it was all about?

But what price were they paying to find such a cure? Was the cure justification enough for the lives of these patients? Were these patients truly just cattle, barely human, no more or less objects to run tests on, problems to be solved, and diseases to be cured?

The truck stopped momentarily, again jolting Viktor.

"Well, here we are, doctor," said the cook's assistant, who gestured with his hand. "The White Stag, just as you ordered."

Viktor smiled and began to get out of the truck. With his body half out, he paused and turned back to the cook. "Thanks a lot for the ride. Say, do you know what time it is?"

The cook's assistant lifted his watch. "It's about fifteen till noon, doctor."

Viktor slammed the door. "Thanks again."

The truck took off to parts unknown as Viktor began to push the door to the White Stag open. A sudden hand on his shoulder stopped him.

"Can you spare some marks for an out on his luck, ex-soldier?"

Viktor turned to find a bedraggled man, unshaven and missing a left arm, directly behind him. The distinct smell of alcohol penetrated Viktor's nostrils.

"What do you say?" The man persisted. "I could sure use a bite to eat. Anything you could offer would be wonderful. Could you help a fellow out?"

Without answering, Viktor shrugged the hand off and stepped inside the pub.

CHAPTER TWELVE

The waitress had begun to seat him at the bar with the other patrons before Viktor interrupted her.

"No," he said. "I need something a little more private, please. Do you have a separate table available?"

The waitress looked put out, but nodded quickly and guided Viktor to a small table bookended by two chairs. "Will this do?"

"Yes. Thank you," Viktor answered as he seated himself, facing the entrance. He wanted to be civil even though he could tell that strangers weren't particularly cared for in towns like Sterlingaart. And he had just been staying at this very inn not too long ago. Oh well, in small towns, you don't stop being a stranger until you've taken up residence for some time, and even then probably not.

The waitress left without asking him if he'd like something to drink. Luckily, he didn't have to wait long for his brother to arrive.

August entered, temporarily filling the dark and smoke filled chamber with sunlight. The light was shut out just as quickly as he closed the door behind him. Viktor lifted his hand to wave, which his brother didn't see immediately. His eyes must have still needed adjusting to the gloom.

Finally, August noticed his brother who sat at the lone table by an abandoned piano. Viktor stood as soon as August drew near.

"Well, about time," said Viktor.

August removed his coat, hung it on an empty chair and sat across from Viktor. "Sorry, I was a little busy…wrestling with God and all that."

"Yes, it must be a lonely life you lead," said Viktor. "But, at least you have God to keep you company. Oh, and that housekeeper. What was her name again?"

"Senta," August said. "I take it you've finally gotten moved into that castle up on the hill?"

"Ages ago. Yes, I've finally gotten away from the nice, warm room at the White Stag for the drafty uncomfortable suite at the Castle Zarfuyls. We doctors practically swim in luxury."

"I bet you do," said August.

They were interrupted by the arrival of the waitress. "Gentlemen, what can I…Father Gottlieb?"

August looked up. "Amalie Schotz. And how are your parents doing?"

"Oh, not so well, father. Da has been out with pneumonia for a full week and ma had to pull extra hours at the mill."

"That's too bad. Do pass on my regards to them. We'll remember them during our intercessory prayer time."

"Thank you, Father. Now, what can I get you gentlemen?"

"Oh, just get me a roast beef sandwich and stein of beer, please," August said.

"The same for me, please," said Viktor.

Amalie nodded and retreated to the kitchen behind the bar.

"So," said August, "how goes the work at the Castle?"

"Oh, it has its moments. In fact, I just had a moment with a particularly violent patient this morning. He threw his tray and started screaming at a wall. I had to hold him down until we could...um, properly restrain him."

"That must have been exciting."

"It was," said Viktor. "And how about you? Had any exciting conversions lately?"

"This is a parish church in a small town, Viktor. To have a conversion, we'd have to have a new family move in. Maybe you ought to send some of the doctors and patients my way."

"I think the Führer might frown on that," said the doctor.

They sat in silence for a moment.

"Look, I'm gonna come right out and say what I've heard and it isn't pleasant," August said. "There are rumors that the patients up in Castle Zarfuyls are being killed. In fact, I've heard that it's not just happening in Sterlingaart, but in several other facilities as well. Your program emptied out all the sanitariums in Germany and is going to exterminate any patient that the Reich considers useless, isn't it?"

Before Viktor could respond, Amalie returned with the sandwiches, which she placed in front of the men.

Viktor raised his sandwich up before his eyes and then dropped it back onto the table. It rocked the plate with its massiveness.

"Just like ma used to make. Enough sandwich to choke a yak."

August grunted and began to eat, like it had been early that morning since he had a drop of food. Viktor shook his head gently as he watched his brother.

"Don't they ever feed you? Or are your parishioners not tithing enough? You know, I remember as a child that you had an amazing appetite. You used to break into the larder all the time and take food. Father used to beat you senseless, but you never learned."

Viktor paused and took a sip of beer, the head of which caught on his upper lip.

"In answer to your question: yes. We are using a series of questions and exercises to determine the fitness of the patients. The Director of Science and Medicine has very strict guidelines about what constitutes a fit patient. All others…"

He let the sentence trail off, the meaning still hanging in the air.

"I see," August said. "And I wonder how many of the patients have actually been considered fit enough to not be exterminated."

"That's not really my area. I've been administering the initial interview, among other activities."

"And what is your prognosis, doctor? Are any of the invalids worthy of life."

"You act as if I enjoy this work, August, but I don't." Viktor lowered his voice and moved in slightly toward his brother, "Look, I honestly don't agree with the wholesale slaughter of all the…the invalids. But what choice do I have any more? You know exactly what would happen to me if I quit the project. I'd go to the Russian front or be carted off to one of the special camps."

"So, you've finally come around to the right way of thinking?"

"Don't be an idiot, August. All I've come around to is the firm belief that there's a difference between a mercy death and this insanity. Yes, I still belief that deaf, dumb and blind is no life whatsoever. Yes, I still believe that most of the invalids would be better off not being born than having to live a meaningless existence. But that doesn't make me a murderer."

"So, what does it make you?" August asked. "You talk about those patients like they're less than human beings. You sound just like the men in charge when they talk of the Jews. They're scum. They're vermin. Their lives are meaningless."

"It's different."

"Not at all. So a man's life is meaningless because…why? Because he can't hold a gun? Because he can't work in the factories? A man lost a leg in the last war and now he can't hold down a regular job. Does that make his life meaningless as well? And what about the old and sickly? When you get to be a certain age, does your life suddenly cease to have any meaning? When did we get to the point where we value a human life's worth depending on how much work he can accomplish?"

"It's not all about what work someone can or cannot accomplish

81

and you know it," Viktor said. "You just want to look at whatever side you want to see and are blind to everything else. What about those who have to care for the terminally ill? What about their families? Do you think it's easy taking care of them? It takes a toll on everyone involved, not only physically but emotionally."

"Life takes a toll on everyone involved," said August. "We were made to carry one another's burdens. We were designed to take care of those who couldn't take care of themselves."

"And did God design those poor souls as well? If so, he should be ashamed of himself."

"'Who gave man his mouth?'" August said, quoting. "'Who makes him deaf or mute? Who gives him sight or makes him blind? Is it not I, the Lord?' Yes, God made man in His own image. And each one is precious in his sight: not just the perfect and normal ones, but God loves 'the world' so much that He was willing to make the ultimate sacrifice."

Viktor began to clap, softly and in slight mockery. "That was wonderful. Was that part of this week's sermon, Father or something you just came up with all by yourself?"

August looked down at his plate. "Actually, we're doing something a little different this Sunday. Do you think you could make it?"

"Mother asked me that same question. They only let me out today and expect me back tonight. But…I'll see what I can do. I wouldn't mind listening to you preach. Once is never enough."

"Dad never got to hear me preach," said August. "Our dear mother, however, has been by every Sunday faithfully. I'll bet she's never been by to see you in surgery."

"Yes. You're the winner. Congratulations."

August caught Viktor's eyes. "Do you really believe that all those children at the castle are miserable and all their lives are meaningless?"

"August, I don't know. All I know is what I've seen and the ones I've been around. Are all of them miserable? I don't know. I know I would be. Would they all rather die or not be born? I don't know the answer to that question either. All I can do is ask myself what I would do in their place."

"I've got a better idea," said August. "Why don't you ask them?"

They ate in silence for a moment, letting the food cool their spirits. For some reason, it was almost always this way when they had a conversation, thought Viktor. If it wasn't the sanctity of life, they'd be forever arguing something. It was August really. He was always in search of a cause.

After a moment of quiet, Viktor spoke. "So, you've stoked my curiosity. Why is tomorrow's sermon different from any of the other quality homilies you've presented in the past?"

August placed his half-eaten sandwich on the plate and looked around the bar. Obviously not finding what he was looking for, he leaned in a bit closer to Viktor. "I have had two important visits this week."

Viktor leaned in as well. "Don't tell me, Hitler wanted you to baptize himself and Eva Braun and Heinrich Himmler wanted you to officiate at his nephew's communion?"

"Don't be an idiot, Viktor. No, my first visitor was a pair actually. The Gestapo showed up at the parish."

Viktor half choked on the bite he was taking. "The Gestapo? What did they want with you?"

"Oh, they wanted me to know that the Führer would not be pleased with the direction I've decided to take with my homilies. They stated, in no uncertain terms, that I might want to reconsider my subject matter before I found myself in a place far removed from happiness."

"And, of course, you chased them out of your house, or, better yet, had that housekeeper chase them out with a broom?"

"They left, all right, but not after assuring me that they would be in the congregation this Sunday to make sure that I uphold my end of the threat."

Viktor took a sip of water. "So, of course, you've decided to preach on the love of Christ or some other innocent topic?"

August gave a wry smile. "Well, that's where things get a bit tricky. My other visitor for the week turned out to be Bishop Eberhart."

August sat back as Viktor attempted to struggle with the significance. "Bishop Eberhart, you say. And who or what exactly is a Bishop Eberhart?"

"He's the Bishop over my diocese," August said. "The man I report directly to."

"I thought you reported to the Pope," said Viktor.

"Yes, thank you for reminding me of your ignorance. I forget that we live in two completely separate worlds. Anyway, Bishop Eberhart came to complicate my life even more."

"That shouldn't be too difficult. Did he give you another orphan or widow to visit?"

"Hardly," August answered. "He did give me a homily that he himself had prepared. Every priest in his diocese will be reading it tomorrow."

"And I take it that this homily isn't about the love of Christ."

"Well, if you mean the disciplinary love of Christ, then yes. Actually, I think you've got the gist of it. It's your typical hellfire and brimstone speech against the Nazis in general and the T4 Program in specific."

"What?" Viktor practically rose from his seat before August reached out to stop him. "Are you insane? You can't read that."

August looked around, probably to see if anyone was watching them after Viktor's outburst. He needn't have bothered. The drunks at the bar were busy drowning their miseries and the waitress was nowhere to be seen. That made sense, thought Viktor. He could have used a refill of beer.

"Of course, I'm going to read it. Every priest in the diocese is going to read it. It's called being one with the body of Christ."

"It's called insanity. The Gestapo already told you that they would be at the service. And what do you think they will do with you once you give this incendiary sermon? Do you think they'll just shrug their collective shoulders and say, Oh well, we can't blame him because it's actually the Bishop's sermon? No. You'll be the example, August. They can't go after the Bishop, but they sure can go after you."

August slowly untangled Viktor's hand, which had fastened on his outstretched arm. "Will you relax, Viktor? Again, if the message is preached in several parishes at once, it has to give them some sort of pause. And I would hope that my own parishioners wouldn't just stand by and let them cart me away."

"So, now you're placing your faith in the peasants of Sterlingaart to save you, is that it?"

"No, I'm placing my faith in God the Father, who had always been there to protect me."

Viktor shook his head slowly. "And what happens if God decides not to protect you this time? What happens if He decides just to sit back and allow the Gestapo to do with you what they want?"

"Well," said August, "as Paul put it: to live is Christ and to die is gain. I'll either be working for Him here on earth or will be with Him in Heaven."

84

"And a fat lot of good that will do everyone else stuck here on this miserable planet. Have you thought any of how ma would take it if her precious August were taken away to be killed or locked in prison forever?"

"Actually, yes I have. I figured that she could come stay with you at the Castle."

"Oh, that's just perfect. And am I supposed to hide her in the closet of the room I share with two other doctors?"

August laughed. "Oh, quit worrying. I'm sure it won't come to that. And if something does happen to me, she can live with Senta. Actually, I'm sure she's quite content to live by herself in our old house."

"Yes, I was by that old shack not too long ago. It looks like it could fall down around her at any moment."

"I have men from the church stop by from time to time to help out if she needs anything fixed. She's not completely defenseless. Anyway, why are you suddenly interested in her well being? Have a change of heart and decided to become a better son?"

It was Viktor's turn to smile. "I haven't been that bad of a son. Sure, I've been busy with college and internship, but it doesn't mean that I don't love my own mother. Do you really think I'm that inhuman, August?"

"No, of course not."

"I'll tell you what. Maybe I was a bit over dramatic with what I said earlier. I'm sure I could get a ride into town tomorrow and witness the Bishop's sermon. Mother would love to have me around to comfort her when the Gestapo takes you away." The grin quickly slipped from Viktor's face. "August, you do realize that there's a good possibility that they will take you away or, at the very least, drag you into their headquarters for a nice, healthy beating. Are you sure you want to put yourself into this predicament?"

"Honestly, and with all due respect Viktor, what they are doing at the Castle and several other sites across Germany to the children is wrong and someone has to make a stand against it. It's the right thing to do."

"Life's not always black and white, August. Sometimes you can get stuck in the gray. Some of us have been there for a very long time."

"Yes, well maybe the gray isn't gray at all. Maybe the gray is just a lighter shade of black."

CHAPTER THIRTEEN

Viktor stepped outside the tavern roughly fifteen minutes after his brother had departed. He had sat at the table in silence, long after his sandwich had been digested, trying to focus and order his beliefs. He hadn't really given his thoughts much thought lately. When he thought of the disabled, he thought of pain, of suffering and of neglect.

When he considered Dieter however, pain, suffering and neglect did not enter the picture. No, there was something special about that boy. He may have been blind, but that didn't seem to limit him. He possessed too much compensation.

Viktor glanced up at the clock embedded in the tower atop the Sterlingaart City Hall. It was fifteen minutes till two o'clock. It didn't seem like he had been in the White Stag for almost two hours. It felt more like a few minutes. Well, he had better get moving. He was supposed to meet Olivia by the train station at two o'clock.

As he walked the streets, Viktor noticed the dead feeling of the city. Granted, most adults were working in the middle of the day, but it was Saturday. Shouldn't there have been a few more people out and about on the city streets?

It wasn't as if the streets were completely deserted. He had noticed, for instance, a strange little man bent over in an alley near the White Stag vomiting profusely. There had also been a couple, husband and wife most likely, who, when passing him, had narrowed their eyes, as if they thought he was a snake. He had brushed that experience off quickly.

He made it to the train station without incident and leaned up against the nearby station house. There were a few people inside the station, waiting on trains. Two soldiers, probably on some sort of leave, were loitering outside, near the tracks, smoking and laughing. An old lady and a young boy sat on the bench outside near the tracks as well. A few others lingered inside the building. But no sign of Olivia yet.

Viktor wondered for a fleeting moment if the agreement to meet him here had been some sort of trick. There weren't a great number of women who had stood up Viktor Gottlieb, but it had been known to happen. And if it happened this time…

A Hansa Borgward 2000, sun gleaming off its silver bumper, glided up to the curb outside the train station and stopped abruptly.

In the passenger side, Viktor could just make out the image of Olivia as she bent over to kiss the cheek of the driver.

Now what was this, wondered Viktor

As Olivia thrust the door open and stepped outside, Viktor glanced inside and noticed the blushed cheeks and bald head of Director Obermayer.

"Viktor," said Obermayer, "you take care of young Olivia now. I want to see her back at the castle no later than seven o'clock."

"Yes, sir," replied Viktor dutifully, as he slammed the door.

The car took off and Olivia was left with a slack-jawed Viktor.

"Do close your mouth, Viktor," Olivia said. "I'm afraid you'll draw attention."

Viktor dutifully closed his mouth and turned back to Olivia. "I take it you are familiar with Herr Director."

"Oh yes," confided Olivia, "I am extremely familiar with Herr Director. Some may even say too familiar."

Viktor narrowed his eyes slightly as he turned to watch Obermayer's car disappear in the distance. "In what capacity, exactly, would you say that you are familiar with Herr Obermayer?"

Olivia laughed, a light, tinkling noise that spread throughout the station, causing the soldiers to glance up sharply in their direction. Instead of answering his question, Olivia grabbed Viktor's arm and led him down a sidewalk, away from the station.

He glanced down, noting her brightly-colored dress and the camera which dangled from a cord around her neck. "Plan on doing some sight-seeing in fair Sterlingaart?"

"Oh, you never can tell when something interesting may just happen."

"Have you been interested in amateur photography for long?" Victor asked.

"Not photography, really," Olivia answered, "But I've had an interest in newspaper writing since I was a child. I don't know where it came from really. My father was into medicine, my mother was a housewife. I guess it just comes from reading mostly."

Viktor stopped suddenly. "Your father is Herr Obermayer."

Olivia grabbed his arm and propelled him onward. "Of course, silly. I thought you knew."

"You thought I knew? How could I know? Your last name isn't Obermayer."

"It was once." She lowered her eyes. "Of course, it changed

when I married Captain Siegfried Kluge."

Viktor stopped again. "One moment, please. You were married to the same Siegfried Kluge who mastered air defenses while flying with the Jagdstaffeln over France? He must be at least twenty years your senior."

"He was twenty years my senior," Olivia said. "It was an arranged marriage and I was very young. My grandfather flew with him in the war and we met a few times when he came to visit. He started coming around more often as I grew older and I noticed how his intentions wavered from my grandfather to me. Not that I minded his intentions. He was twenty years older, but he was still trim and had excellent mental facilities. When I turned seventeen, we were married."

"But I thought I heard..." Viktor caught himself by the time his sentence was half out of his mouth.

"That he died? Yes. On one of the first missions the Luftwaffe ever flew, his plane was shot down somewhere over Poland. They never recovered his body."

"I'm sorry for your loss." Viktor hesitantly asked, "How long had you been married?"

"Just under two years. Oh, we wanted to have children but the war just wouldn't allow it. That's why I was free to come with father to Castle Zarfuyls."

"And, are you enjoying your job here, at the castle?"

Olivia looked wistfully at the river as they passed. "It's just a bit sad."

Suddenly, a loud voice rang out behind the couple. "I want to know what happened to my son!"

Viktor and Olivia turned quickly to see an older couple moving toward them. The man was taking great strides to catch up with them but the woman seemed to hold back a touch, perhaps wanting something but also not wanting to intrude either.

Viktor immediately recognized both of them as the older couple who had stopped his brother after the service he had attended. He hoped desperately that they didn't recognize him.

"You two work at the castle?" The old man stated.

"Sir?" Viktor asked.

"I want to know what happened to my son. You had him up there and he never came back. They said pneumonia like that explained everything. But they lied. I know it."

"Gregor," said the old woman, pulling at the man's sleeve.

"No, Maria, I'll have my say. Now, what have you done with his body? And what did Kolger really die from? I don't believe pneumonia for one moment. And you can't tell me otherwise."

Gregor, the old man, stopped for a moment as tears began to course down his cheeks. "Why did you do it? He was my only son. My only son. He didn't deserve to die. He was a happy boy. He loved his father and mother and never hurt anyone. He was a good boy. Why would you kill him? Why?"

Viktor reached out to the old man. "Sir, I don't know..."

His hands were slapped away. "Don't sir me. You don't earn the right to call me sir. I don't want your respect or your pity. I just want my son back."

Maria grabbed her husband and pulled him gently but firmly toward her. His words gone, he allowed himself to be comforted by his wife.

Olivia stepped toward the old man and his wife. "I don't know if I knew your son, sir. But I can assure you that I haven't killed anyone. I am sorry for your loss."

The old man's face softened slightly. "Thank you for your kind words, young lady. I...it's just that there are so many questions. And all we know is the Gestapo came for our Kolger and then we received word that he was gone."

"I understand perfectly, sir," said Olivia sweetly. "I would be upset as well. After all, he was your only son. You loved him very much and he died so suddenly."

Gregor nodded. "That's right. And we did love him and we miss him."

"Of course you do," Olivia cooed. "Any loving parent would. I am sorry about the loss of your son. Please accept my condolences."

Gregor allowed himself to be pulled away by his wife. After they had rounded a corner, Viktor and Olivia continued on their way.

"That was very impressive," Viktor said.

"What was?"

"The way you soothed that couple back there. I thought he was going to start a fight in the street."

"Oh, you learn how to soothe a lot of frayed nerves as a nurse. It just comes as part of the scenery really. I've had to deal with parents suffering the loss of their child many times. It's never easy, but the important thing is to get them moving. You get someone focused on anything but the immediate situation and the pain becomes that less acute."

They came to a bridge that spanned the river.

"So, did you know their son?" Viktor asked. "I never heard of a Kolger. But, then again, I'm not really encouraged to find out a lot about these patients."

"No, it's better not to become too familiar with these patients, isn't it?"

Viktor stopped at the top of the bridge. "What do you mean?"

"Well, all the ones I've seen have some kind of physical or mental deformity. You just know that there's no way they'll pass the standards of usefulness of the state. I mean, have you seen them? The majority of them can't even tie their own shoes or brush their own teeth. What sort of life is that? It's meaningless."

Viktor became silent and stared at the river flowing under him. He remained that way until Olivia touched him on the shoulder.

"What are you thinking about?" She asked.

"You reminded me of something I said earlier. I was talking with my brother and I said something about how being deaf, dumb and blind is no life at all. My brother asked me if I thought their lives were meaningless."

"Well, of course their lives are meaningless. I mean, what sort of life can you have when you have to live that way? I would rather be dead. I don't know about you, Viktor, but I haven't seen a single patient at that castle that wouldn't have been better off not being born. What can they do? What can they accomplish? Can they serve Germany as our young men go off to war? All they can do is steal our resources that are badly needed elsewhere. They're a liability and that's all."

Viktor reflected quietly for a moment as the wind blew a large leaf across the bridge and into the waters beneath them. Finally, he stretched his body and looked directly into Olivia's eyes.

"I wonder if we'd think differently if it were us."

"I don't..." Olivia started.

"My brother asked me what they would say if I asked them if their lives were meaningless. And I really can't say. I want to think they would agree. I believe that they would be able to see how much of a...a liability they were to Germany, to the war. But I really don't know. If they thought their lives had meaning, does that make us wrong or does it make them delusional?"

"Well, it's just as you said, Viktor. If they can't see the damage they're doing to their own Fatherland, then maybe they're the ones who are delusional. Maybe they're just being selfish. But I really don't think any of the patients I've seen would want to live given the chance. I really couldn't fathom that at all."

Viktor shook his head. "I'm sorry. This must be incredibly boring for you. I had my head in this topic thanks to my brother and I haven't been able to get out all day. Forget the patients and forget the castle." He grabbed her hand. "My lady, the beautiful hamlet of Sterlingaart awaits. What exotic adventures would you enjoy?"

Olivia smirked, as she was led from the bridge. "This is Sterlingaart, after all. What sort of exotic adventures could there be?"

* * * * * *

As it turned out, there weren't any exotic adventures to be had at all in the small hamlet of Sterlingaart. Certainly, the two marveled at the barbershop, the post office and city hall. The river surrounding the city was certainly lovely and at least the weather was being hospitable. They spent an hour or so at the park that was located in the heart of Sterlingaart.

When the sun began to sag noticeably in the sky, they went in search of a restaurant. They wound up at the White Stag.

After they had been seated for several minutes, the waitress appeared at their table.

"Well, couldn't get enough the first time?"

Viktor looked up at Amalie. "And you're still at work."

"It's a blessing and a curse." Amalie replied.

After the waitress had taken their order, they were left alone.

"So, you were telling me about your brother," Viktor prompted.

"Well, of course I was. Yes, Julian was always the fastest, always the smartest, always the favorite. It was very amusing when he told father that he wanted to sign up for the army. Father objected and mother made a scene in front of some guests that happened to be present. All in all, a very enjoyable evening."

"I'll bet. And where is your brother now?"

"That's the sad part. About a year and half ago, Julian was released from active service and returned home rather unexpectedly. We received notice beforehand of his condition. Still, it came as quite a shock to us all. Apparently, he and a few members of his squad had wandered while engaging the enemy. Fighting was fierce

91

and the bullets were flying and Julian and his fellow soldiers were running for their lives. The next thing he knew, the bullets stopped and there was this awful calm. He looked around to find out that they've wandered into the middle of a minefield.

"They attempted to retrace their steps, but, of course, someone stepped on a mine and then another one. After all the explosions, there was only Julian and one other fellow left and I won't tell you what they were covered in, although Julian gave me all the gory details. Julian and this other soldier noticed that they were only a few steps from the sign signaling the end of the minefield. Julian was about three feet away so he decided to jump the rest of the way. He bent his legs, made a giant leap and landed two feet beyond the sign. But someone must have either moved the sign or planted a mine outside because he landed right on one.

"Luckily, because of the forward momentum, the mine only blew his legs off instead of killing him. When he came home, everything below the right knee and the left thigh were missing. It was a devastating blow for mother and father."

"I'd say," agreed Viktor. "And who takes care of Julian now?"

"Mostly mother. She dotes on him day and night, like he was still her little baby. Meanwhile, I'm stuck with father on the T4 program. He needed a nurse who wouldn't get squeamish or sentimental and he knew he could trust me."

"Oh, you're the tough one, eh?" Viktor asked. "Well, thank goodness you're brother made it back alive. There's twenty dead for every one that comes back alive, or so I've heard."

"Yes, my family was certainly thankful of that," said Olivia. "And, your brother. You've told me about him, but you haven't told me what he does. I take it he lives somewhere here in Sterlingaart."

"Yes, he does. I went to visit him when we first arrived here. He lives in this charming little house on the outskirts of Sterlingaart, right beside a small brick church. He's the parish priest."

CHAPTER FOURTEEN

They took a taxi: Sterlingaart's one and only cab, back to the castle long after dark had settled in. Both had imbibed a few too many drinks and were leaning on one another for support like a pair of drunken college classmates. Every other minute, Viktor would whisper something in Olivia's ear, causing the nurse to break out in gales of laughter.

The driver glanced annoyingly in his rearview mirror but decided to hold his tongue. After all, these two must be staff at the castle and it never paid to speak harshly to those who were held in high esteem by the Reich.

After a long trip through a dark countryside, although not long enough for Viktor, they arrived at the castle. Having paid the driver, Viktor offered his arm to Olivia.

Olivia shook her finger at him. "Oh, no, no, no, Viktor. That would not be seemly, would it? Can't have two staff members openly fraternizing, can we?"

Viktor frowned. "I guess not."

"You can, however, do me the pleasure of walking me to my room."

Viktor and Olivia took off through the maze-like passageways of the castle, attempting to move quietly. More often than not, however, they ran into objects and ended up giggling down every other hallway. In one hallway near the kitchens, they passed Captain Oster, who peered at them suspiciously, but didn't attempt any conversation.

They arrived at Olivia's door without incident.

"Well, Olivia, I want to thank you for a very enjoyable time. Thank you for taking the time out of a very hectic schedule to accompany me through the fairy tale land of Sterlingaart. May I call on you again sometime, young lady?"

Olivia giggled softly into the back of her hand. "Of course, Herr Gottlieb. But why so rude? Isn't it customary to make certain a lady's apartment is clear of all brigands before leaving her safe and sound at her castle?"

"Frau Obermayer, excuse my incompetence. I am, after all, an idiot."

So saying, Viktor turned the knob and swept the door open. He quickly stepped inside and turned on the light overhead, illuminating the room. It was a sparsely furnished room, devoid of anything but the most essential of needs, such as a bed, a small writing desk with an accompanying chair, and a wardrobe.

Viktor turned back to her, sweeping his arm grandly. "Your suite, my lady."

She curtsied to him. "Thank you, good sir."

He allowed his eyes to travel over her room, resting finally on her. "So, it must be nice having a room all to yourself. Nepotism sure has its benefits."

Olivia closed the door behind her and moved toward the desk. "Nepotism has only a little to do with this, my young, handsome doctor. I would prefer the company of some fellow nurses. I requested it, actually." She opened the top drawer of her desk and removed a bottle and two glasses. "But the rooms were full when I arrived. Daddy insisted that I take this room."

At the mention of Herr Obermayer, Viktor swung his head toward the door.

"Oh, don't worry about him, Viktor," Olivia said as she began to pour the liquor into the small glasses. "Daddy is never up this late. Like a good man, he retires at precisely eight every night."

Holding a glass in each hand, Olivia moved toward him. "You, however, are not a good man and therefore must pay the ultimate penalty."

Taking the glass she offered, Viktor knocked it with hers, making a sharp cling in the otherwise soundless room. "Here's to nepotism."

Olivia smiled, taking a sip.

* * * * * *

Early the next morning, while the majority of the castle remained sleeping, Viktor slipped out of Olivia's room, closing the door softly behind him. He was almost certain that she was still asleep, as her gentle breathing seemed to indicate. He had to hurry and get back to his room, change and bathe if he was going to make it to his brother's church later this morning.

Not that he was in any way thrilled with listening to an hour-long sermon delivered by his brother.

He'd already had to undergo one of those ordeals. But, of course, his mother would be disappointed if he didn't show. It seemed like she was always disappointed about something or other. One would have thought that becoming a doctor would make any mother proud, but there was always room for criticism.

94

Viktor careened through the hallways of the castle, careful to be as quiet as possible. His head throbbed like he had a toothache and he was sure that his eyes were extremely bloodshot as well. They certainly felt like they were on fire. His stomach threatened to rebel, but some bread and a shower would bring him back to wholeness again.

Viktor arrived back at his room to find Konrad on the ground by the door, wrapped tightly in a blanket and snoring. Viktor reached down to shake him awake.

"Konrad! Konrad, wake up!"

Slowly, Konrad's eyes creaked open. "What? Who is it?"

Viktor stood. "It's me, Viktor. What are you doing sleeping outside the room?"

Konrad shook his head. "It's Robert. He locked me out last night."

"He what?"

"I arrived here later than usual after a pretty long day of interviews to find the door locked. I knocked on the off chance and Robert answered from inside. I asked him to let me him, but he refused."

"Why didn't you just get a guard to let you in?"

Konrad smiled sheepishly. "I didn't want to get Robert into any trouble. Seems like he's been losing it lately, going a little off. So, I thought I'd give him a break just this once."

Viktor smiled back through the headache. "So where'd you get the blanket?"

Konrad held it out in front of him. "Rescued it from the patient's linen closet. I didn't think they'd miss it much."

"Aren't you worried about lice?"

Konrad scratched his head absently. "I didn't think about that."

"Well," said Viktor, "let's get this over with." He turned and banged on the door. "All right, Robert, prank time is officially over. Open up!"

Silence answered him so Viktor knocked again.

"Come on, Robert! Open up!"

With no answer again, Viktor took a step back then quickly brought his foot up to smash into the doorknob. The door quickly swung open. Konrad stared at him.

"Former Gestapo training," Viktor answered. "I'm joking. The clasp on our door is extremely old. I've been meaning to have it

95

replaced."

The first thing they noticed on entering was the extreme cold of the room, due to the open window. The second thing they noticed was the complete lack of Robert.

Viktor turned to Konrad. "Are you sure he was in here?"

"His voice was coming from inside this room," said Konrad as he moved toward the window to shut it. "So unless he's a trained ventriloquist, which I'm almost certain he isn't, he must have..."

Konrad pushed down on the window but it wouldn't close the entire way. He gestured at Viktor. "Turn on that lamp, will you?"

Viktor moved to switch on the lamp. Once additional light hit the room, the men could make out a rope tied to the frame of Viktor's bed that led out the window. The bed was pulled slightly askew and into the middle of the room.

Konrad looked a silent question at Viktor, who moved to the window and slammed it open. He bent his body slightly out the window so he could look directly under the sill. And there, swaying slightly in the wind, hung the lifeless corpse of Robert Schessmacht.

* * * * * *

Later, Viktor and Konrad received a full grilling by Captain Oster and Herr Obermayer. Several orderlies had been by to remove Robert's slightly bloated corpse.

"So, Doctor Werner, you stated earlier that Robert had locked you out of the room. Why did you not alert the guard immediately?"

Konrad sat on the edge of his bed, his chin in his hands. "I told you, I just didn't think about doing that. I was tired. I just wanted to go to sleep."

"And you'd rather sleep in the hallway than go to the trouble of getting a guard to unlock your room?"

"Yes," said Konrad.

Oster wrote something quickly down in his notebook before turning to Viktor. "And you, Doctor Gottlieb, were not here at all. Where were you last night?"

Viktor, who stood by the desk, folded his hands over his chest. "Is this a murder inquiry?"

Herr Obermayer walked over and placed his hands on Viktor's shoulders. "Please, Viktor, we just need to gather this information as soon as possible to allow everyone to get on with their lives."

"Of course," Viktor answered. "I was in another room of the castle...with a nurse. We were talking most of the night."

96

"And which nurse would that be?" Oster asked, with a slight gleam in his eye.

"You know which nurse that would be, Captain Oster. Why ask me these idiotic questions?"

"And that would be the same nurse I saw you wandering the halls with at a later part of last evening, would it doctor?"

"Of course," Viktor said through slightly clenched teeth.

Obermayer, for the most part, seemed oblivious. "Viktor, you know the rules against fraternization among staff while here in the castle. There will be consequences."

Viktor bowed his head slightly toward Obermayer. "Of course, sir. I understand."

Obermayer turned to Captain Oster. "Certainly you've finished for now, Captain?"

Oster closed the top of his notebook. "Of course, Herr Director."

With a quick sidelong glance at Viktor, Oster left the room.

Obermayer moved to sit at the chair by the desk. "Gentlemen, I realize you've been through a very traumatic experience as Robert was a friend to you both as well as a good colleague. I want you to take some time out today to refresh yourselves in whatever manner you need. Unfortunately, I can't grant you any additional time away as we are on a very tight schedule."

Viktor raised his hand tentatively. "Sir, my mother asked if I could accompany her to church this morning. Do you think that would be possible?"

Obermayer pulled out his pocket watch and glanced at the time. "Shouldn't be a problem. But make sure you don't make a habit out of it. You know how our Führer feels about the patently religious."

"Of course, Herr Director. It's just for my mother's sake."

Obermayer stood and stared directly into Viktor's eyes. "And remember exactly what I stated about staff fraternization while you are under the roof of this castle, Herr Gottlieb. It will not be tolerated under any circumstances. Do I make myself clear?"

"Yes, Herr Director."

Obermayer smiled slightly. "Good."

The Director walked to the door, then stopped and turned back to the men. "One last thing, doctors. Do any of you recall anything out of the ordinary in the last week or so with Robert? I'd hate to think that we saw the warning signs but did absolutely nothing to help."

Viktor looked at Konrad, who shrugged.

"I don't recall seeing anything out of the ordinary, really." Konrad answered. "He was quieter than usual, I guess. With our busy schedules, we don't really have time to be sitting around analyzing each other."

"I don't expect you to either," Obermayer said. "What about you, Viktor?"

"I don't believe I noticed anything completely out of the ordinary, sir. It's really hard to say. We work in a place where ordinary isn't ordinary. Maybe I got so used to seeing unstable individuals that I didn't see the signs right in front of me."

"Perhaps." Obermayer smiled gently at them, in his best imitation of a grandfather. "Well, hopefully this unfortunate event won't darken your spirits too much, gentlemen. Of course, this may mean that we load up your caseloads just a bit more. But I'm sure you can handle it. Well, get some rest. Director's orders."

As soon as Obermayer left, Viktor heaved a sigh of relief. "That was close."

Konrad shook his head. "Yes, I don't know why, but it feels like I just dodged a bullet, even though I did absolutely nothing wrong. And just who, exactly, is this lucky nurse, Viktor?"

"Don't even ask," said Viktor, rolling his eyes. "So, how are you doing, Konrad? I know I'm still a little shaken up."

"To tell you the truth, it hasn't touched me deeply. I wasn't friends with Robert. I don't think he even liked me for some reason. So, besides still seeing his purple face continually in my head, I don't think I'll lose much sleep over this."

Konrad leaned in a little toward Viktor. "I'll tell you a little secret, Viktor. All of this, everything we're doing here at the castle, it all seems like I'm walking through some sort of dream. I mean, none of it seems real, so it doesn't really touch me. You know? I just keep waiting to wake up."

"Maybe you will someday soon, Konrad. I don't know. For me, Robert taking his own life hasn't really sunk in yet. Maybe it never will. But I understand what you're saying about a dream. I feel like a child acting like an adult sometimes. I act like I think an adult should act and do what I'm supposed to do, but I feel a little drugged. I feel like I do things but it's not really me that's doing them. The real me is watching from somewhere far away."

Suddenly, Viktor stood and headed toward the door. "I've got to go or I'll be late."

"Are you really going to church, Viktor? At a time like this?"

"I promised my brother I would."

* * * * * *

Viktor caught a ride into town from the cook's assistant again. Luckily, he caught the man just as he was heading out the courtyard in his truck.

"Hey," yelled Viktor, stopping the vehicle. "Do you have room for one more?"

The Cook's Assistant reached over and popped the door open. "There's always room for one more, doctor."

As soon as Viktor entered the cab, the Cook's Assistant thrust the truck into gear, jerking it down the road.

"So, where to this time, doctor? Going back to the White Stag again for a decent meal? Although, I've got to tell you that I tried several meals at the Stag since we've been here and most have been lacking. I don't know what they're paying their cook, but they need to raise the pay, fire the one they have and hire a new one."

Viktor eased himself back into the seat. His headache had just about subsided, but was still resting on the surface, as if threatening to pound in fury at any moment.

"I think I'm going to church today."

The Cook's Assistant shrugged. "Suit yourself."

CHAPTER FIFTEEN

Luckily, Viktor arrived at the parish house in plenty of time before service started, so he decided to see if his brother had time for a talk. He had to knock on the door several times before it was answered.

The housekeeper, Senta, cracked open the door with a frown pasted firmly on her lips. "Yes, can I help you?"

"Yes. I wanted to know if I could talk with my brother, August, before he had to start service. Normally, I wouldn't bother him right before he had to speak, but I...something's come up."

Senta's face lightened up immediately. "Of course, dear. I'm sure he'd be happy to listen to you for a few moments. But only a few moments, mind you. He can't be late to service."

"Of course," Viktor answered.

He edged into the house and Senta began to guide him back to the study. "Now, keep in mind that he's got an awful lot on his mind right now. Are you sure this couldn't wait till after?"

"It's just...something's happened and I'd like his opinion on it."

Senta nodded as she walked past the kitchen. "Of course, dear. I completely understand. Wait here for one moment, please."

The housekeeper left him outside the door to the study. Viktor could hear some furtive whispering before Senta arrived back at the door.

"He said he'd be pleased to talk with you as long as you understand his time constraints."

"Certainly," said Viktor.

The doctor entered the study to find his brother, vestigial robes hanging loosely off his shoulders and hunched over some papers on his desk.

August gestured toward the empty chair in front of the desk. "Viktor, have a seat. I'm afraid I don't have much time to spare this morning." He glanced at a clock on his desk. "I've only got about ten minutes actually."

Viktor took the offered seat. "This shouldn't take too long. There's just something that happened this morning and I thought you might be able to...I don't know."

August smiled warmly at his brother and sat down in a chair. "Tell me what's going on?"

"One of my fellow doctors, a friend, hung himself right outside

100

our room window last night. And I just…I don't know. I thought you might be able to…" Viktor shrugged.

"Was this friend of yours a Christian?"

Viktor glanced up sharply. "What? Why should that make a difference? He's dead."

"I was just curious, Viktor. I'm sorry for your loss. I understand that this must have affected you deeply. Would you like me to pray for you?"

This suggestion surprised Viktor into affirmation. "Sure."

Both men closed their eyes as August began. "Gracious Father in Heaven, I bring before you my brother who has had the very traumatic and sad experience of having someone very close to him take their own life. Father, comfort my brother as you alone know how and bring your will and glory out of this situation. Father, help use this unfortunate incident to bring everyone involved closer to you. If anyone should not have a relationship with you, please allow this tragedy to lead them to you. In Jesus name I pray. Amen."

August looked up to find Viktor staring at him. "I come to you for comfort and you use this time to try and sell me on your religion?"

"That's the only comfort I know, Viktor. What did you want me to say? He's in a better place? At least he's not suffering? He's with God now? How can I say that when I don't know anything about the man? You wouldn't want me to lie to you, would you?"

"How do you know it would be a lie?"

"How do you know it wouldn't be?" August shot back. "I didn't know anything about the man. According to the Bible, only those who trust God to save them will go to Heaven. For me to say anything else would be for me to deny the validity of God's word."

Viktor sat back and crossed his arms over his chest. "If that's what the Bible says then your God must be very selfish indeed. I mean, how can He just pick and choose who goes to Heaven and who doesn't? Are you saying my friend wasn't good enough for your precious Heaven? Are you saying that he was somehow underneath your God's standards?"

"Isn't that what you're saying about the children up at the castle? No, sorry about that. That was unfair. I'm just a little concerned about this morning's service. I apologize Viktor. You're right. You came to me for comfort and all I can do is give you the opposite. Look, let's talk about this after the service when I have a little more time for you."

Viktor dropped his eyes. "You're right and I'm sorry as well. I didn't mean to be antagonistic. I came to you after all. It's not your fault that you're answering as you normally would."

August smiled and patted his brother's hand. " I really am sorry for your loss, Viktor, and if there's anything I can do, please don't hesitate to ask."

Viktor smiled back at his brother. "Thank you, August."

* * * * * *

Viktor noted the two Gestapo in the crowd as soon as he entered the sanctuary. It was hard not to miss them. They wore their uniforms proudly. One was a small, bald-headed fellow, lean and trim while the other was a hulking brute, probably the enforcer of the group. August had better be careful when dealing with these two.

Viktor gestured for his mother to enter the row in front of him just as the curtains opened and August entered.

August stepped forward, straightened the pages out before him on the lectern and cleared his throat.

"Let us pray," the priest intoned as he closed his eyes.

The snaps and clicks of the prayer boards being released echoed throughout the sanctuary as the parishioners bent down in prayer.

"Oh God in Heaven," said August, "we are so weak and need your strength every day. Please look down upon us with your favor. Please lead us and direct us in your paths and not ours. And please open our eyes so that we may see your glory. In the name of the Father, the Son, and the Holy Spirit."

"Amen," the congregation recited as they rose once more from their knees to their seats.

As August straightened out the pages, Viktor glanced at the Gestapo. They appeared extremely alert, almost as if they were looking for open signs of rebellion.

"Fellow laborers in Christ, we are going to treat you to a different sermon today. Bishop Eberhart came to see me earlier this week and presented a message that all of the parish churches in his diocese will be presenting this morning. So, please enjoy this message from our very own Bishop Eberhart."

August bent his eyes down and began to earnestly read.

"In the beginning, after God created the Heavens and the earth, He gave man his first directive. Take care of the garden. Not long after, it was take care of the animals. Then, take care of your helper and your family. All through the Bible, God gives and gives graciously and what does He ask in return? Does He demand all our money or everything that we hold precious? No. He only asks that we care for what He considers precious. He asks us to be His caretakers.

"You can see God's love all throughout the Old and New Testaments. 'Thou shalt love thy neighbour as thyself.' 'He doth execute the judgment of the fatherless and widow, and loveth the stranger, in giving him food and raiment.' 'And when ye reap the harvest of your land, thou shalt not wholly reap the corners of thy field, neither shalt thou gather the gleanings of thy harvest. And thou shalt not glean thy vineyard, neither shalt thou gather every grape of thy vineyard; thou shalt leave them for the poor and stranger.'

"There is only one commandment that runs the gamut of the Bible from start to finish and that is, 'Verily I say unto you, Inasmuch as ye have done it unto one of the least of these my brethren, ye have done it unto me.' And who are the least of these? Who can be more 'least of these' than the sick, the downtrodden, the cripple? And who does God command us to care for above any other: the sick, the downtrodden, and the cripple. In other words, take care of those who cannot care for themselves."

Viktor eyes traveled over to the Gestapo. He could tell that they were becoming agitated and wished his brother would hurry and get the message over with. Whatever outcome this event had to face, let it hurry up and get here.

"A baby comes into this world," continued August, "alone and defenseless and teaches its parents during the first few years of its life the most essential commandment of God: take care of those who cannot take care of themselves.

"Jesus Christ, our God and Savior came down from Heaven where He reigned as king to walk this earth as the lowliest of servants. And whom does our Lord surround Himself with the most: the sick, the sinner, and the cripple. He came down to Earth and He debased Himself to take care of those who couldn't care for themselves."

Viktor wondered to himself why God, if God loved the weak and helpless so much, why He couldn't help them Himself. Why did He, an all-powerful God, need people to do His work?

"We Christians have many jobs: to evangelize, to spread God's love, to build up one another. But the central tenet of our faith is simply this: take care of those who cannot care for themselves. We are the hands and feet of our Lord and Savior, left here to complete His job. We even lead others to Christ because their own sinfulness has blinded them and they cannot care for themselves. They need someone to walk alongside them and lead them to salvation. They need someone to take care of them.

"Our worth as human beings neither starts nor ends with how others perceive us. If that were truth, then no one would be worthy of Heaven. No one is that useful to God. For God created us, we did not create Him."

And that, thought Viktor, was where the church parted with reality from the rest of the world. Everyone else does weigh a man or woman by their usefulness.

"Think!" August practically shouted. "Does God only love the useful or the normal? No, of course not. 'For God so loved the world, that he gave his only begotten Son, that whosoever believeth in him should not perish, but have everlasting life.' God sent His Son to the world. God did not send His Son only to the normal or to the perfect. After all, 'They that be whole need not a physician, but they that are sick.'

"Right now, in towns across Germany, a great evil is being perpetrated against the ones God considers most precious: the innocent and defenseless. Right now, the Reich is rounding up the invalids: the sick and the cripples. The ones they deem too useless or unworthy of life, they are destroying. They are murdering the ones who cannot take care of themselves: the very ones we are commanded to care for. This madness, this murder, this sacrilege against the most basic of God's commandments must stop!"

A parishioner shouted aloud, "Amen!"

And it was at that point that the Gestapo, the burly one, almost rose to his feet. Viktor saw the smaller man pull the larger one back into his seat, then whisper something furtively into his ear. The larger one nodded back.

"Fellow Germans, I implore you to stand firm in the face of such open belligerence against the righteous commands of our Lord and Savior. I plead with you to stand for what is right and decent. And I beg you to take care of those who cannot take care of themselves."

Viktor could tell, though, that it wasn't simply the Gestapo that were getting agitated. Little groups sprinkled throughout the crowd

104

were speaking to one another in hurried whispers. A couple further down the bench from where he and his mother sat were openly discussing the injustice of the situation. They were speaking so loudly, in fact, that the smaller Gestapo turned his head to glare at them. They continued on though, despite the obvious threat.

There were several shouts of "That's not right" and "They're killing our children" as the parishioners surged to their feet in preparation of being dismissed. Viktor could feel the tension of the crowd as if a massive storm cloud were gathering strength right in the small church. Besides his mother's bewildered looks, his face was the only other one that seemed to not be snarling.

As they departed the church, Viktor could hear snippets of conversation from those around him.

"It's time we do something about this," a small bearded man said from in front of him.

The lady next to him agreed. "But what can we do about it?"

"Well, I don't know about everyone else, but I'm going to bring this up to the Mayor."

"That's right," said another man next to the couple. "We still have our say in this government, even if they did put some thugs in charge. They have to listen to us."

Few of the parishioners stopped to greet August as he stood by the door. Apparently, they were immersed in their own angry worlds.

When Viktor reached August, he shook his head slightly. "You've really done it this time."

"It wasn't my doing," August countered. "This was entirely the Bishop. But if it achieves the desired result, then it will be worth it."

"And what result is that?" Viktor asked. "To get you thrown into prison?"

August shrugged as Viktor moved to stand a few feet away. He still had a conversation to finish from this morning. The parishioners, for the most part, had disappeared into small groups and gone their separate ways, many of them still fuming and discussing ways they would appeal to the government. Good luck with that, thought Viktor.

"Viktor, can you walk me home please?" His mother asked.

"Of course, ma," said Viktor. "Wait one moment while I go tell August. I want to make sure he's here when I get back."

Viktor stepped back to the front of the church just in time to catch August addressing the Gestapo.

"Inspector Lowe and Kriminaloberassistant Zimmer. How pleasant of you to come to service today."

"I can honestly say that I am very disappointed in you, Father Gottlieb," The smaller Gestapo said. "I had such hope that you would choose the correct path, but alas, it was not to be. As we all know, wide is the path that leads to destruction, Father. Now, we can't touch the Bishop because of his contacts and position. But we can certainly touch his priests. Father Gottlieb, expect us to be in contact with you very shortly."

The two men left without another word.

Viktor entered the church just as soon as he knew the Gestapo were well out of sight. "You've really called down the thunder now, August. Or maybe it was your Bishop that called it down on top of you."

August smiled to his brother as his hands rested on the pew in front of him. "Oh, it doesn't matter who started the fire, does it Viktor, as long as the weeds get burned away?"

"So, what are you going to do when they come for you because it sounded to me like you won't have long before they do just that?"

"Oh, you heard that, did you? Yes, while Zimmer can be physically threatening, Inspektor Lowe seems to make up for his diminutive size with the appropriate verbal threats. I don't worry about myself. I know God's in control of the situation. I just pray that no one else gets hurt."

"And what if that happens? What if your fiery Bishop's message gets a whole lot of your townspeople so worked up that they decide to do something stupid and end up getting hurt or worse? What if it ends up getting you killed?"

August smiled again, the perfect martyr. "To live is Christ and to die is gain, eh Viktor?"

CHAPTER SIXTEEN

For whatever reason, Sundays were usually quiet events at the castle. There was no logical explanation. The patients and staff were still very much in existence, as most went nowhere for church. But some sort of peace fell on the castle and it was usually a very relaxing day for Viktor. As soon as he returned, he let the quietness wash over him as he went about his routine.

His parents had forced him and his brother to attend church when they were young. It was not an obligation: it was a right. But when he had left their house, he left behind more than just their presence. He left their rules and traditions behind as well.

There were some familial leftovers, however miniscule, that he still performed subconsciously. He still felt the center of a door before opening it. When Viktor had been three, there had been a fire, contained to one room. Viktor had been the one to discover it, grabbing a violently hot doorknob that had been heated from the opposite side. He would never enter a room without testing it first.

And then there was the polishing of his shoes. He always polished his shoes by rubbing first seventy-five times clockwise, followed by seventy-five times counter-clockwise. He had forgotten the time his father had picked him up and set little Viktor on his workbench and spent a full hour and a half teaching his son how a man polishes his shoes. Of course, that event was buried so deep in the subconscious that it would take an army of miners several years to dig it out. They were just quirks that he never even realized that he was forced to live with.

It was his fastidious habit of shoe polishing that led him down into the depths of the dungeon on that quiet Sunday, looking for a can of black shoe polish. One of the guards, Werner he believed was the name but wasn't certain, had advised the young doctor that somewhere down two stories below the castle, besides a plague of rats, one could find, if one looked hard enough and with due diligence, a supply room that contained, among other hidden treasures, a can of black shoe polish. If Viktor could possibly wait until three that afternoon, Werner would be happy to escort the good doctor down to that exact room.

Viktor enjoyed the release that the polishing offered, allowing his mind time to work through Robert's death and his brother's sermon. The only problem was that Viktor had been on clockwise swirl number twenty-three, and the habit was so deeply ingrained in him that he had to have that fresh can now so he could complete his ritual. It wasn't simply a want. Viktor desperately needed to complete the job.

Which was why Viktor now ambled cautiously through a centuries-forgotten part of the castle, where surely no person had set foot in God knows how long. Dust covered everything like a newly birthed snow. Luckily, he could follow his own footsteps back the way he had come if necessary. In fact, he had reached the point of frustration when he was about to turn around and go back the way he had come when he heard the scream.

It was female or simply high-pitched and coming from somewhere farther down the hallway. As soon as it started, it cut off, almost as if someone had stepped on the person's neck and forcibly stopped the scream short.

Viktor paused imperceptibly, then rushed down the hallway. Normally, he wouldn't have bothered, but the voice sounded feminine and whoever she was could be lost or in some sort of danger. And it could be Olivia.

He walked quickly past a massive, ironbound door and halted. Viktor cocked his head, alert for any other sound, but heard nothing. And then he noticed one other queer fact: the floor in this part of the castle wasn't covered with a thick layer of dust. It had been used often enough to require sweeping and general repair.

As he took a cautious step forward, a lone noise, metal crashing against metal struck his ear and caused Viktor to turn toward the door. The door handle wasn't rusted like the ones he had passed farther down the hall. He reached out and grabbed it, turning it easily.

The door opened and an unmistakable shaft of electric light fled through the crack and lit up Viktor's face. Confident, he tensed to swing it open the rest of the way and was stopped by a voice not five feet from him inside the room.

"No, you idiot, leave that cloth where it's at. My headache can't take another of her screeches."

"Yes, Herr Doctor," came the soft reply of an orderly that Viktor vaguely recognized.

"Close her cage, will you? I'm very much done with her today. I'd like to catch a look at the one with the boil though, after you're finished."

Viktor again heard the sound of metal, perhaps a door locking, and then a sound as if a heavy object were being dragged across the floor. He attempted to peer through the crack but was only rewarded with a view of a nearby wall.

"No, lock the cage as well," The Doctor said. "Can't have our little beauty escaping, can we? God, I hate being here on Sundays. Doesn't Obermayer understand a day of rest? Well, it's needed, I can assure you. If he continues running us like we're animals, then that's all he'll have left: a pack of wild animals. Probably a pack of broken animals after we're through. Yes. Number Thirty-Two, please."

After a few more sentences, Viktor finally was able to recall the owner of the voice: a certain Doctor Jorg Braub or Braun. He'd only met the man once, at the beginning of his stay at the castle. He'd been introduced to Braub or Braun by Obermayer.

Braun/Braub was a small fellow with a long goatee and a long mane of hair to match, which was odd to see on a doctor or scientist in the Reich. Usually they preferred professionals to be as clean cut as their military. Perhaps this doctor was the exception.

Someone behind Viktor cleared his throat.

He turned quickly and noticed the shadowy visage of Oster, the Captain of the guard, standing further down the passage. The Captain stared at him for a moment before speaking. "Are you lost, Herr Gottlieb?"

Viktor's mind raced furiously. In one respect, he would like to be gone from this place as soon as possible and he certainly didn't want the Captain to believe that he was snooping around in places where he shouldn't have been. On the other hand, he would desperately like to know what sort of experiment or exercise was being performed in the room. His curiosity proved stronger than his sense of self-preservation and he produced a quick lie. After all, he was a doctor, and that should be enough to get him out of most messes.

"Herr Obermayer sent me down here with a message to Doctor Braun," said Viktor, thinking fervently, please let it be Braun and not Braub.

Captain Oster considered this bit of information and then tilted his head toward the door. "Well, don't just stand there, listening at the door. Please go in."

"Of course," Viktor answered, pushing the door open and flooding the hallway with light.

It took a moment for Viktor's eyes to grow accustomed to the glare of electric lights in the room. The main area was lit up like the interior of a surgical area by several hanging lamps. In the center of the room, where the orderly stood hunched over a figure in a chair, was a long table filled with all manner of surgical implements, scalpels and syringes, along with more common instruments, such as a hacksaw, a small sledge hammer, and ice tongs. Interspersed among these instruments were vials of oddly colored liquids and hypodermics, some filled while others lay empty.

A few feet away from the chair was what looked like a cross, affixed into the cement of the floor. Manacled chains hung from each cross beam where the hands would go and a thick, iron ring was screwed into the center.

The far wall, however, immediately attracted the young doctor's attention, as it was filled with row upon row of dog kennels filled with patients. Some were fully dressed in white gowns while others went naked. But all were covered in filth and had a metal and leather apparatus around their heads, which prohibited them from speaking or making any noises.

The orderly finished his last knot and stepped away from the chair, which held a young man strapped at his hands and feet. Some sort of rash or abrasion ran the length of the left side of his body and his eyes darted constantly around the room in terror. He was dressed only in a cloth that covered his midsection.

Doctor Braun turned an instant after they entered and his eyes lit on Captain Oster. "Ah, good Captain. What can I help you with today?"

The Captain inclined his head toward Viktor, who smiled hesitantly.

Herr Braun frowned in return. "Yes? What is it?"

"Herr Obermayer requested that I come down here to observe you in your work today, Doctor Braun."

"Oh, did he?" Braun turned back toward the table. "Well, this isn't a medical school. I have serious work I'm attending to here. I don't need someone looking over my shoulder as I complete my research. You can tell Obermayer that for me."

"Yes, Herr Doctor," said Viktor.

Braun selected what looked like a paint scraper and a pair of pliers and stepped toward the young man strapped to the chair, whose eyes were extremely frantic now.

"Ritter," said Doctor Braun, "get a bag."

The orderly hurried over to the table and grabbed a black plastic bag and hurried over to assist the doctor. Meanwhile, Captain Oster had wandered over to a nearby table and was leafing through some random pages on the desktop.

Braun attempted to thrust the scraper under the metal and leather helmet on the boy's head with little to no success. He finally threw his hands down and grabbed the bag from Ritter's hands.

"It's no good." The doctor said. "We're going to have to take off the mouth guard."

Oster, unbidden, moved to close the door as the orderly released the straps that held the helmet in place. The moment the helmet was sufficiently loosened, the patient began to shake his head from side to side and howl miserably. Viktor's hands shot straight toward his ears.

As soon as he had deposited the mouth guard on the nearby table, the orderly returned to the doctor's side. Braun attempted to use the scraper on the side of the boy's face, but the constant thrashing made it impossible.

"Hold his head!" Braun ordered.

The orderly stepped behind the chair and grasped the patient's head firmly with both hands until the shaking was barely perceptible. The howling, however, continued.

As soon as he was able, Doctor Braun brought the thick metal instrument up and began to glide it down the boy's face as if he were shaving him. When the metal touched each pustule, the boil burst and yellowish liquid ran down toward the patient's neck. The howls turned immediately to screams of pain.

Viktor glanced down and noticed the Captain standing directly beside him. In his out-stretched hand were two yellow earplugs.

"You'll need them if you plan on staying down here for too long."

Viktor took the plugs and immediately began to stuff them in his ears. "How is it that we can't hear this in the main part of the castle?"

The Captain shrugged. "The door is a natural sound barrier as well as the walls around this area of the castle. Plus, we're three floors below the cafeteria. I'd be surprised if you could hear a small explosion from down here."

Viktor turned back in time to see Braun pulling a small white worm out of one of the pustules in the side of the patient's face.

111

After tugging the worm free, the doctor dropped it into the bag opened on the table. He immediately set about digging the pliers into another broken pustule as the orderly struggled to hold the patient's head steady.

The young doctor turned back to the Captain, who was smiling grimly. "How did that boy get infected with those white worms?"

"The maggots?" The Captain asked. "Who do you think placed them in his face to begin with? It's just another of Doctor Braun's little experiments. I guess they figure that the patients are going to be put down anyway, so they may as well see what makes them tick. They can only research so much on the dead ones. Live test subjects are so much harder to come by."

Viktor turned his eyes away from the Captain and the scene being played out before him. He needed to clear his mind for a moment and he needed to get out of this room into some clean air before he went mad. His eyes traveled over to the cages and locked with one of the patients in the middle row, a young woman with an enormous boil on her neck.

As he stared at her, it seemed as if she was trying to send him some message with her eyes. She was, or at least had been, quite beautiful at one time. But now, her straight black hair was clipped close to her head and black circles lined the bottom of her eyes. The boil vibrated slowly, like a beating heart. She gripped the bars of her cage and stared solemnly out at him, pleading with him.

If Martin had been there, he could easily have told Viktor who that young, still striking girl was. However, even Martin may have been hard pressed to recognize Louisa, the Spanish beauty now. Her uncontrollable laughter had finally been terminally silenced by Doctor Braun.

"That's enough," cried Doctor Braun. "Put that cursed helmet back on quickly. I can only stand so much of his howling for one day."

Viktor felt a callused hand drop on his shoulder.

"Come, Doctor Gottlieb," said Captain Oster, "out into the hallway with me for a moment."

Viktor glanced warily at the boy with the open sores running down his face. "Of course."

Once out in the hallway, Viktor offered the ear plugs to the Captain. Oster smiled and shook his head.

"No, thank you, Herr Gottlieb. I have no need of used earplugs.

You keep them. You never know when they might prove handy." Captain Oster dropped a not-too-friendly arm across Viktor's shoulder. "Now, how about you explain to me what you are doing in this part of the castle?" Viktor shrugged off the Captain's arm, feigning indignantly. "I told you just as I explained to Doctor Braun. Herr Obermayer requested that I come down here to observe."

Captain Obermayer smiled coldly. "And we both know that Herr Obermayer would never have directed you down here to observe Doctor Braun. He barely allows you to initially interview the patients. Now, why are you down here?"

As Viktor opened his mouth to explain his story, a young guard rounded a nearby corner at a trot. Seeing Captain Oster, the guard slowed but continued.

"Captain Oster! Captain Oster! Your presence is required immediately, sir."

Captain Oster forgot all about the young doctor and turned his full attention to the guard. "Yes? What is it?"

"Sir..." the guard glanced hesitantly at Viktor.

"Just out with it, guard." Captain Oster said.

"Sir, we've received word from Bruntmeister general command. Apparently the populace in Sterlingaart and other surrounding towns are openly protesting in the streets. As the only military presence available, we are commanded to Sterlingaart with all haste."

The guard and Captain Oster started down the hallway. As they reached the corner, Oster turned back to Viktor.

"Doctor Gottlieb, would you be so kind as to join us for a moment. I would still like to hear your story and I would appreciate you close by me at this time."

"I really don't have the time for this, Captain," said Viktor.

Captain Oster revealed his humorless smile again. "If you would prefer, doctor, we could go up to Herr Obermayer's office directly and inquire of Herr Director."

"That won't be necessary," said Viktor as he hurried after the two.

CHAPTER SEVENTEEN

Captain Oster led Viktor down a series of twisting and turning passageways, past a few guards that hurried around them like worker bees busy running a hive. They exited through one last door into the castle's massive courtyard, where several guards scurried around a diesel truck.

There was another car, parked but still running, off to the side of the truck. Leaning against the front of the car was a portly figure dressed in simple business attire, who straightened as soon as he noticed the two men.

"Captain Oster," said the man, "it's about time. I've got a crisis here and the Reich promised me your full assistance."

"And you'll get it, just as promised, Mayor Fenstermacher. Now, tell me about this emergency."

Mayor Fenstermacher looked from Oster to Viktor. "Who's this?"

"Your emergency, mayor?" Captain Oster repeated.

The Mayor fidgeted with his cigarette case. "Yes, well, it appears a certain priest in my town has inflamed the populace with a fiery sermon damning your operation. Right now, a good-sized crowd has gathered in front of City Hall to protest."

"And you want us to kill them?" Oster said.

"Hardly. No, I plan on going down there to address their concerns and send them home. But I would like some armed guards accompanying me just in case."

"In case you succeed in irritating them enough so they take out their rage on you instead of us, eh? No need to answer that. Do you know if anyone in the crowd is armed?"

The Mayor's hands trembled as he shoved the cigarette into his mouth. "I don't know. I left as soon as the crowd grew to about ten people."

Oster looked around at his guards, then nodded at the Mayor. "You'll get your armed escort, Herr Mayor. Give me five minutes, please."

The Mayor nodded back to the Captain, threw his cigarette down to the cobblestones, where it lay smoking, and re-entered his car.

Oster turned to one of the guards who stood next to the truck. "Lieutenant Klum, please take the good doctor here and have him outfitted in a guard's coat and rifle on the double."

114

Lieutenant Klum reached forward and grabbed Viktor's arm, which the doctor promptly shook free. "Look, Captain Oster, this has gone far enough. I'm a doctor, not a guard or a soldier. And I'm not going anywhere with you…"

Captain Oster pointed a finger directly at Viktor's nose. "You listen to me, doctor. You will go anywhere I say and do anything I tell you to do. I am going to keep an eye on you for a little while until I can find out exactly what you were doing in my basement. So, you will come with us and be a temporary guard for me. Besides I may need an extra man."

"This is ridiculous," said Viktor. "I'm not going to go anywhere except straight up to Herr Obermayer's office and tell him exactly what is going on. And don't think for a moment you'll be a Captain much longer."

Oster moved forward, his nose scant inches from Viktor's. "You may have forgotten, in between your years at college and your years at interning, that you still belong to the State. You will do exactly what the State requires you to do every minute and every day. Don't for a moment think that you're any better off than those pitiful patients, because you're not. You and I will do what we're told because we don't have any say in the matter. If the Führer requires that you take off your doctor's coat and replace it with a guard's coat, then you'll do it because that's what the State requires of you. If the State wants to honor you, it will. If the State wants to send you to the Russian front, it will. And if the State wanted to exterminate you and toss your rotten corpse in a ditch, it would do that as well. Don't think for a moment that because you are a doctor that you have greater freedom. If anything, because of your position and responsibility, you have an even greater responsibility toward the State. Don't ever forget that, doctor."

Oster turned once more to Lieutenant Klum. "Again, Lieutenant, I require that you take Doctor Gottlieb to the guard room, outfit him in guard's attire, arm him and bring him right out here again. You now have two minutes."

Lieutenant Klum threw out a hasty salute, grabbed Viktor's arm and thrust him toward the guardroom.

* * * * * *

A few minutes later and the doctor, formerly garbed in hospital whites, now stood decked out in a guard's jacket, combat shell on his head and a rifle in hand. In spite of the change of clothing, the

115

expression of deep irritation had yet to leave his face.

"Don't think that you won't be hearing about this as well, Lieutenant. I want you to know that I'll be giving a full report to Herr Obermayer about this outrageous situation as soon as we return."

For a response, Lieutenant Klum continued to walk, head slightly down, until they had come to the rear of the truck. He motioned toward the open rear flap and the tailgate, which had swung low and was built with deep grooves to enable effortless climbing.

"After you, Doctor Gottlieb."

Viktor grunted, threw the rifle over his shoulder and began to climb. As soon as he had gained the level ground of the truck bed, he turned for one last shot at the Lieutenant.

"And don't think for one moment…"

The Lieutenant slammed the tailgate closed.

The young doctor, finding no convenient outlet for his aggressions, felt backwards, found the wooden seating on the side of the truck and sat backwards, grunting. After a moment, his eyes adjusted to the interior gloom and he noted several guards sitting on the wooden bench, beside and in front of him. Most of them sat with eyes glued to their boots, except for one guard sitting next to Viktor, who smiled widely.

"So, I haven't seen you around here. New, are you?"

"Not exactly," answered Viktor.

The window between the front and rear of the truck slid open.

"I will need absolute quiet from now until the time we arrive back at the courtyard," came the unmistakable voice of Captain Oster. "You are not to speak a word, even if spoken to, do you quite understand, gentlemen?"

The men answered with silence, even Doctor Gottlieb, who thought, under the circumstances, that it would probably be the most prudent road to take.

Oster continued. "There will also be no firing of weapons. We are simply along to provide support to the Mayor. This is not a conflict situation. These are innocent civilians. That command includes you, doctor."

The window slammed shut once more and the truck took off.

"Ahh. I was really hoping we'd see some action," said the guard next to Viktor.

Viktor could only look out the rear of the truck and watch the road to the castle as the great stone structure began to dwindle in the distance.

* * * * * *

They arrived in the center of town twenty minutes later. The tailgate was thrown open and Lieutenant Klum whispered urgently from outside.

"Come on, let's go."

Viktor, the last to get up, was the first to come down. He looked toward the sound of the crowd and could just make them out, having to shield his eyes from the setting of the sun. He was roughly pushed in the back.

"Don't be rude, doctor." Oster said. "Didn't your precious mother ever tell you that it's not polite to stare?"

Captain Oster motioned with his jaw and Viktor fell in line behind the other guards who were making their way up the stone steps. Once at the top, the men turned and lined up behind the Mayor, who was talking to a short, obviously irritated man. Viktor recognized the man as the one who had recited the verse from the Bible at August's church.

Viktor noticed his own hands holding the rifle were trembling slightly just as Captain Oster passed behind him. His father's voice repeated a warning in his head, telling him not to handle a weapon unless he was ready to kill.

"You nervous, Gottlieb," whispered Oster. "Don't worry, they're only townsfolk. You could probably take out two or three of them before they were on you. Maybe four."

Viktor began to sweat even though the weather was turning a bit cooler due to the setting of the sun. Now the small man was yelling at the Mayor and had him gripped by the lapels of his suit. Viktor turned his head toward Captain Oster for directions.

The Captain advised them to stand their ground while he stepped down toward the Mayor. The crowd, in response, surged forward up the first step and Viktor could visibly see the anger in their eyes. He recognized the older couple who had confronted Olivia and himself yesterday in the city.

A shot rang out and his eyes were drawn immediately toward the Captain, who, with a smoking pistol held straight up toward the sky, was yelling to the people, telling them to disperse and return to their homes. This halted the mob on the steps, but didn't dismiss the anger in their eyes.

The sweat from Viktor's forehead traced a trail down his eyebrow and into his left eye. Still holding the rifle, he raised his arm and wiped the sweat away with the back of his hand. He could feel his palms sweating as well as he temporarily lost the grip on his rifle.

Suddenly, the small man lunged at the Mayor and Captain, yelling something. Viktor's entire body tensed in response and he heard another shot, this one somehow distant yet close by as well, and felt the rifle kick in his hands. The small man seemed surprised at first, then slowly began to shrink down into himself as he slipped to the ground.

As the crowd quickly dispersed The Mayor and Captain Oster marched up toward Viktor, leaving the dead man on the steps below.

"Who gave you the order to fire, soldier?" Mayor Fenstermacher asked.

"I didn't mean to do it. I swear I didn't. When he jumped at the Captain, I tensed and..."

"It's okay, doctor," said Oster. "You probably saved us a great amount of trouble."

"Saved us trouble?" The Mayor fumed. "Are you insane? Do you realize the amount of repair this will take? I'll be busy for weeks to come fixing the damages this idiot did. Did you say he was a doctor?"

"That's right." Oster said.

"Look," started Viktor, "I told you I didn't want to be here. I've never even handled a gun and now look what you did. When I get back to the Castle there'll be a full report of this incident sent to Herr Obermayer instantly."

Captain Oster bent down and placed his face so close to Viktor's that the doctor could smell the faint reek of alcohol on his breath. "No, you listen to me, Doctor Gottlieb. It was you that pulled the trigger and it was you that took an innocent man's life. Now, if I were you, and I'm not, thank God, but if I were, I'd be coming up with some sort of plan of explaining your way out of this mess."

"This is blackmail."

"Whatever it is, it's all yours."

Captain Oster turned from Viktor and the Mayor and walked back down the steps toward the truck. "Men," he called as he marched, "time to move out."

"I don't know who you are, young man," said the Mayor, "but

118

you've done enough damage in my town for one day. You need to leave."

Viktor, head hung low, strained down the steps toward the awaiting truck.

* * * * * *

It took longer to get back to the castle then it did to get down. As they exited the paved road that led out of town for the dirt and gravel road to the castle, they stopped suddenly. A sheepherder from the neighboring farmlands had decided to lead his flock directly across the road.

Viktor found himself sitting next to the same guard that he had traveled next to down to the city. This time, however, the guard remained astutely quiet; occasionally glancing up at the doctor when he thought the man wasn't looking.

He had taken a man's life today and didn't quite know what to think about it. He was shocked but mostly he was outraged at Captain Oster who had placed him in the center of this mess. Yes, he had been in a part of the castle he probably had no right to be in, but so what? Was his punishment to be forced into a situation where he had no choice but to fail? What kind of choice was no choice?

Viktor looked out the open tailgate at Captain Oster, who was currently yelling at the sheepherder, to no affect. What was that man doing at the castle? He should be somewhere on the front, leading the charge. It's what he seemed to want.

Viktor didn't know if he half blamed the mob back at City Hall. They had a right to be scared. They had a right to be outraged at the way their government was treating their children and loved ones. Did they have any rights when it came to their children? Didn't they have a say in whether their children should live or die?

Now, he was all for ending pain and suffering. If a patient elected to die instead of live through agony, that should be their choice. But what choice did those at the castle really have? What choice was no choice?

Viktor had no idea and he didn't think he had any answers any more. Madness was madness no matter which way you looked at it. And what they were doing didn't seem much like helping their fellow Germans any more.

Soon, the end of the flock appeared and they were able to continue on their way.

119

CHAPTER EIGHTEEN

Viktor hadn't traveled too far from the vehicle depot located on the side of the castle when a figure stepped out of the shadows and into the hallway in front of him.

"I heard that you enjoyed a trip into the city tonight?" Olivia said.

Viktor nodded. "Hijacked is more like it. Oster and his brutes forced me to go as they were a man short. I plan to file a full report with your father first thing tomorrow morning. They can't just..."

"Oh, I don't know if I would do that, Viktor."

Viktor cocked his head. "Why? Do you think it's right for the security to kidnap doctors, who should be about serious work and force them to become soldiers?"

"No, of course not. It's just probably not such a wise idea to cross Captain Oster. Even though father's in charge, he still defers to Oster in certain matters. I think there are matters that Oster is privy to that father has no clue about. I think he prefers it that way."

Viktor waved a hand. "Forget it. There's no harm done. So, were you looking for me for anything in particular?"

"I, uh...I heard about Robert."

They started off down the corridor.

"Senseless business, isn't it?" Viktor asked. "I mean, I don't know what happened to him. He started complaining about hearing voices then started acting a little off. I wonder if he picked up crazy from one of the patients around here."

Olivia stopped. "You can't, can you?"

"No, you can't develop insanity from being around the insane. You don't have to worry about that. I think Robert had something else eating its way through his mind. Is that what you're worried about?"

"What do you mean?"

"I mean," said Viktor, "that you obviously haven't got to whatever it is you really wanted to talk with me about. So, out with it. Is this about last night?"

Her shoulders slumped. "Yes."

"Are you worried about being caught or is there something else?"

"I'm a grown woman, Viktor Gottlieb and can do as I please. I have absolutely no fear of being caught, as you put it. No, I just...what happened shouldn't have happened. We both drank way too much and things got slightly out of hand. Now don't mistake me. I like you. But what if I got pregnant, Viktor? What if I should get pregnant? What then? I'm in no hurry to get married because of a one night fling."

"Are you?" Viktor asked.

"Pregnant? I don't know. I wouldn't know for a while. I just wanted you to know that if I found out I was, I would do whatever I needed to terminate the pregnancy. I have too much to do right now and a baby would just complicate things."

Viktor found himself getting irritated despite the fact that he mostly agreed with her. "So, is that what I am to you as well, a complication?"

"It's not you, Viktor. It's me. I have absolutely no wish to ever become a mother. And I certainly wouldn't want to get pregnant by someone I barely even knew. I just wanted to tell you that I don't normally do that sort of thing. It was impulsive and that's not like me."

Viktor stopped and grabbed her shoulders. "Look, Olivia, I wasn't asking you to marry me when I invited you down with me to Sterlingaart. In fact, I had no idea how the day would turn out. Would I like to see you again? Certainly. I think you're beautiful, funny and extremely intelligent. But I don't want to be a father right now either. I'm not sorry for what happened and if there are consequences later on, we'll just have to deal with them. But for now, I'm exhausted. A friend of mine has killed himself, I was in the middle of a riot and I killed someone, so I'm a little bit taxed at the moment."

Olivia was aghast. "You what?"

"When Oster took me down to Sterlingaart earlier, they put a rifle in my hands for some unknown reason. I haven't held a gun since I was a child and that ended in tragedy. I was sweating and nervous and I guess I accidentally pulled the trigger. Someone was hit and the crowd dispersed. I didn't mean to do it."

Olivia cupped his jaw line in her hand. "Oh, Viktor, how terrible for you."

"It's...I don't know. It happened and I don't really know how to feel about it. I mean, it was an accident. I didn't shoot him on purpose, but I can't get the thought out of my head that I should have been able to stop myself and couldn't."

Olivia dropped her hand. "I've been thinking a lot today too and decided that maybe we should quit seeing each other for a while.

Keep the relationship between us strictly professional. At least until we get out of this place. It's not a healthy environment."

Viktor stared into her face before answering. "Okay. Whatever you think is best. Honestly, I'm just too tired right now to even think straight. If that's what you want, Olivia, that's fine."

Olivia smiled quickly at him. "I think it would be best for now. I...we'll talk soon, Viktor. I have to go."

She left quickly before he could say anything else, which was probably for the best. Viktor didn't think he could have continued that conversation if he'd wanted.

Slowly, he plodded down the hallway, not allowing his mind to concentrate on any certain event. Too much had happened in the last twenty-four hours. His mind hadn't processed it all yet.

A large shadow crossed his path, temporarily blocking out the light. Viktor looked up to see Dieter, mop in hand, standing in the center of the hallway.

"Doctor Gottlieb, this is late for you, sir."

Viktor smiled despite his weariness. "Dieter, shouldn't you be in bed yourself at this hour?"

"Oh, they let me out if they have some detail they'd rather not do themselves. In this case, there was a major spill in the women's bathroom that needed some extensive mopping."

Dieter cocked his head and continued staring at Viktor through his sightless eyes. "I wanted to talk with you a moment anyway, Doctor Gottlieb."

"Oh? What about?"

"I heard about your friend, Doctor Schessmacht. I just wanted to say that I'm sorry for your loss. I know that I'm only a patient and all, but if there's anything I can do for you, just ask."

"That's very kind of you, Dieter. I don't know what to say."

"You don't have to say anything, sir. I didn't say what I did to hear you say thank you. Sometimes people have to do the right thing no matter what circumstances surround them. In this circumstance, you've lost a good friend and the right thing was to offer my condolences and offer any assistance I could."

Viktor stared at Dieter for what seemed like an hour.

"Doctor, are you okay?"

Viktor shook his head. "I'm sorry, Dieter. I'm just tired, I guess. A lot has happened over the last few days. I need some sleep."

"Of course, doctor. Have a good night."

Viktor began to pass Dieter until a thought stopped him. "Dieter, if you could have one wish, would you wish to be able to see?"

"You know, I've thought about that one a lot, doctor. A blind boy would, you see. What if I could not be blind? If there were an operation that would give me back my sight, would I take it? What if there was a magician that came along and offered me my sight back? Who wouldn't want to see if the opportunity came up? Who would be that senseless?

"But then I thought that there are a lot of people in this world who have closed their eyes on purpose because they chose to ignore the world around them. They've voluntarily blinded themselves because sometimes ignorance is the best defense. Sometimes, when you can't deal with the truth, you chose blindness instead. It's a lot better than having to take responsibility for everything, especially things you ultimately have no control over.

"But I was born this way. In certain ways, I'm better off than most people. I've never seen the world outside, so I don't know what I'm missing. I've never seen a sunrise or the sky. I have no idea what my face looks like or my mother's face for that matter. There are a lot of things that I haven't missed out on because I didn't know I had the option of missing them."

"So," said Viktor, "are you saying that you would have chosen to be born blind?"

"None of us can choose what life gets to throw at us, Doctor. We just get to choose how we'll react. I haven't had the best life. I've been beaten and neglected, made fun of and taken advantage of. My mother abandoned me to a sanitarium at an early age because she couldn't take care of me. The doctors and nurses have been the only parents I've known. But, despite all that, if I had the choice of being born blind or not being born at all, I know which I would choose."

Dieter moved to the side of the hallway. "You have a good night, Doctor Gottlieb."

With a grunt, Viktor passed Dieter and continued on his way.

* * * * * *

Viktor made it back to his room without further interruption. He opened the door to a fully dark room. As not to disturb Konrad, who was more than likely asleep, Viktor shut the door slowly behind him and crept toward his bed. Intending to sleep fully clothed, Viktor halted halfway across the floor when the lamp on the desk was suddenly switched on. Captain Oster sat on the chair.

123

Viktor groaned and threw himself onto his bed. "Can't this wait until later, Oster? Haven't you tortured me enough for one day?"

Captain Oster didn't smile. "I have a little mopping up to do first, Gottlieb. I came here because I wanted to make sure you understood the situation exactly."

"And where's Konrad," asked Viktor. "Did you kill him?"

"I sent Doctor Werner on a little nightly errand so we could be alone."

"How thoughtful of you," Viktor said as he sat up on his bed. "So, what exactly do you want, Captain Oster? I'm sure you're not here to tuck me in bed."

"You're quite right. I'm here to find out what your intentions are concerning this evening. Are you still intent on reporting to Herr Obermayer my actions?"

Viktor rubbed his forehead, which was now almost pounding. "I've decided not to discuss the matter with the Director, Captain. I feel that it would be in my best interest if we just kept quiet on the whole matter."

"I agree fully, Doctor. But I do want you to know that I will be watching you very closely from now on. Walking around at night with a nurse, being in a part of the castle that you have no authority to be in and sneaking into locked medication cabinets in the dead of night are all very suspicious activities. If I were you, I would keep a very low profile, Herr Gottlieb, a very low profile indeed."

"And, is that all you wished to see me about, Captain Oster?"

"Just as long as we understand one another, Doctor Gottlieb."

The door swung opened, admitting Konrad Warner, who looked quickly over at Viktor before turning his attention fully on Captain Oster. Konrad handed him a stack of items.

"Here are those bandages you wanted, Captain Oster and the antibiotics. Really, I don't know why you came to me when you should have just gone to someone on the night shift."

Oster took the proffered materials and stood up. "Thank you, Doctor Warner. I had other business to attend to in this area of the castle and appreciate your immediate assistance."

"That's not a problem at all. Did you say earlier that someone had been shot? You really should have the man see a doctor on the night shift. Even if the man had simply been grazed, it needs to be looked at."

Oster turned his head to Viktor. "Did I say that someone had

124

been shot? I'm sorry, I must simply be tired. No one was shot, doctor. Now, gentlemen, if you'll excuse me…"

Oster marched to the door and exited, leaving Konrad staring quizzically at Viktor. "What was that all about?"

Viktor rolled his eyes and fell back onto his pillow. "Ask me tomorrow?"

Konrad shrugged and reached to turn off the light.

CHAPTER NINETEEN

The next morning, Viktor, exhausted from lack of sleep, wandered into the cafeteria in search of breakfast. As he stood in the staff line, he happened to glance up at the doctor's table and immediately noticed Herr Drammels, that bastion of morality from the Reich Committee for the Scientific Registering of Serious Hereditary and Congenital Illnesses, had returned. He was sitting next to Herr Director Obermayer and the pair chatted animatedly like a couple of robins on a tree branch.

Viktor sighed inwardly, knowing that his arrival would mean nothing good.

After slopping what slightly resembled breakfast onto his plate and grabbing a steaming cup of coffee, Viktor made his way through the patients and up toward the dais.

"Doctor," said one of the patients as he passed.

He stopped to look down and noticed Dieter Himmelbach sitting at one of the tables, looking, if he could look, directly at him.

"How did you know it was me?"

"Your shoes," said Dieter. "They give off an odd two-toned squeak. Plus, you use an amazing amount of after shave that sends a cloud out four feet in front of you."

Viktor laughed slightly and moved on.

While still in the process of being seated, Obermayer turned fully on the young doctor with a shrewd expression on his face.

"Doctor Gottlieb, you remember Herr Drammels, don't you? From the Reich Committee?"

"Actually," Drammels broke in, punctuating every word with a stab of his fork, as if he were fencing, "I've been promoted. Or demoted. Or whatever they call it when you get paid the same but gain more work and a new title. I am now Head of the Science and Medicine's new Congenital Investigations Division. A pretty title regardless."

"Herr Drammels is here on official business from the Führer himself," said Obermayer.

"Of course. And I was just about to discuss the news with your Director here. It won't hurt for you to know as well. I'm sure you can't keep secrets like this one for too long around here. No, the Führer has declared that the T4 program be halted immediately. Apparently there was no little chaos from some of the more boisterous Catholic groups this weekend and the Führer has reconsidered the importance of the program. Although, if you ask me, he's just bowing to papal pressure. The whole country's being absconded by the political process, if you ask me."

Drammels stabbed down on a chunk of sausage and plopped it into his mouth as he continued. "Well, regardless, you're to shut down this facility immediately, today if possible. In addition, the Führer requests that you destroy as many of these" he pointed at the patients with his fork "as possible before you go."

Viktor's eyes immediately turned to locate Dieter amid the other patients. He was sitting by himself, oblivious to the world around him.

Obermayer, who had been in mid bite, began to cough spasmodically as a speck of food found its way down his air pipe. Viktor quickly passed him a drink, which he gulped down.

"There must be close to three hundred patients left here," Obermayer said. "How can we possibly get rid of all of them by today?"

"That is not my concern, but yours," said Drammels.

"Why can't we just take them back to their old facilities?" Viktor wondered.

Drammels laughed. "And start this entire mess all over again? Whose side are you on, boy? No, the more of them gone, the stronger off Germany will be. The Führer may have to bow to the will of the people, but we certainly don't need to."

Drammels turned to Obermayer, who still looked a bit pale. "You may want to try an old trick they're using down at Schloss Hartheim. They've attached a hose to the tailpipe of one of their ton and a half trucks and piped the carbon monoxide into a chamber filled with patients. They can take out as many as twenty or more at a time. You may need to do something like that if you're to leave any time soon."

Viktor found his eyes drawn again to Dieter. Would they gas the blind boy as well? Is that how the Reich treated everyone it had no more use for, with a blanket, everyone loses approach?

Then a thought came, un-bidden to his mind, almost as if placed there by someone else. I have to save that boy. He can't die like the rest. Viktor had no clue where the thought had originated, at least he thought it hadn't come from himself, but he clung to it like a drowning man clutching a tree branch.

127

But the real trick would be how to get the boy, unseen, out of the castle. Then what would he do with him? He didn't really know. He'd have to take it one step at a time.

He turned to see Herr Obermayer staring directly at him. "I'm sorry, sir?"

"Viktor, I realize it's quite early in the morning, but wake up please. We have a serious amount of work to do."

"Yes, sir. I'm sorry, sir."

"Now, I'll need you to gather a master list of all the patient's names that are left alive at this facility. I'll need it in one hour."

"Certainly, sir."

As Viktor quickly finished his breakfast, he overheard Obermayer. "Captain Oster, please advise Doctor Braun that he'll need to clean out his little menagerie as soon as possible. I want him working on a carbon monoxide chamber within the hour."

Viktor shoved a crust of bread into his mouth.

"Doctor Gottlieb, are you still here," Viktor turned to find Obermayer staring at him. "I thought my directions were quite clear. You now have fifty-eight minutes to compile your list."

Viktor grabbed his glass of orange juice and fled.

"I don't know what's gotten into that boy," Obermayer said.

"He may have to be eliminated anyway, sir," said Captain Oster. "I received a call from the Mayor about an hour ago and some of the town's officials are calling for his blood. Apparently they want some recompense for the shooting. They demand a sacrifice, if you will."

Obermayer shook his head. "That's most unfortunate. He had such promise. And Olivia will be crushed. But, there will always be casualties in war, right? Oh, by the way, please post guards at each exit to the castle. I'd hate to see the Führer's reaction if we let even one of these patients escape."

Captain Oster rose and bowed slightly. "Of course, Herr Director."

* * * * * *

It took Viktor less than thirty minutes to compile his list. After all, the machine had been quite proficient up to this time. There were slightly less than 300 patients left in Castle Zarfuyls. Who could guess the official body count, but Viktor estimated that at one time, there must have been close to three thousand patients moving between the castle's walls. Yes, they had been quite effective.

By the time he approached the two hundredth name on the list, Viktor had formulated a rough plan. He would disguise Dieter and sneak him out of the castle. Of course, the countryside was wide open from the castle into town. But there would be no chance of commandeering a vehicle. It was out of the question.

From there, he had little to no idea. He could take the boy to his brother. Maybe August would know what to do with him. He was a priest after all. They had a duty to take care of the orphans, widows and the like. Plus, he was bound to have some sort of connections. Perhaps Dieter could be smuggled out of the country.

Confident that he had the outline of a plan, and a very rough plan at that, Viktor hurried along the corridors in search of Dieter. When he filled out the roster of names earlier, Dieter had been lined up with a group of other patients in the cafeteria.

Viktor entered the cafeteria, scanned it quickly and saw no patients. He marched over to the nearest staff member.

"The patients that work in here," asked Viktor, "where are they now?"

The worker, who had apparently been busy scratching his nose, straightened up as soon as he saw it was a doctor addressing him. "Sir, they just left five minutes ago. I believe they were told to go back to their rooms and clean up. Then it's right on the buses for the lot of them. Suppose our jobs over then, eh doc?"

Viktor walked away without answering.

* * * * * *

Dieter wasn't in the dorms. Because of his lack of personal possessions, it hadn't taken him any time at all to pack up. As such, he was the fifteenth patient standing in front of the entrance to the newly constructed carbon monoxide chamber. They stood, lining the walls, with their belongings at their feet. A guard standing outside the chamber raised his rifle as Viktor approached.

"Dieter Himmelbach, I'm glad I found you," said Viktor. "What are you doing here?"

"Sir?" Dieter asked.

"You haven't finished your job with me yet, boy."

The soldier approached. "Sir, can I ask what you're doing?"

"Guard, I need this patient for a few minutes. He left a job unfinished in my office and I'll need him to complete it before he boards the bus."

"Can't you get another patient for the job, sir?"

"Sadly, no. This one has a certain amount of strength that I'll need to move the cabinet around with. I'll just be a moment."

The soldier lowered the tip of his rifle but continued to look doubtful. "Captain Oster's orders were very direct, sir. Once a patient enters this line, they have to move through that door. No one can come get them, except for Captain Oster himself."

Viktor had to think fast. "Look, I've already talked with Captain Oster about this. He said it was okay as long as I brought the patient back here within the hour. And that's all the time I'll need."

"Well, sir, if you've already talked with him…"

"And I have, so everything's in order. Grab your things, Himmelbach."

As soon as they had rounded a corner and were out of earshot of the guard and other patients, Dieter whispered furtively, "Sir, what's going on? Where are we going?"

Viktor stopped and drew the patient into a shadowed alcove. "Dieter, they're going to kill you right now. We've received orders to exterminate the remainder of the patients today and clear out of this facility."

"I know, sir."

"What? How could you know?"

"I already told you, sir. I have acute hearing. I overheard Captain Oster talking to one of the guards. I know all about the carbon monoxide chamber."

Viktor stared. "Then what are you doing just standing there like a sheep? Don't you want to live?"

"Sir, what good would struggle or attempting to run accomplish? How far could I get? I'm blind, remember. Of course I want to live, but what choice do I have?"

"Let me worry about that, Dieter. Come on."

Viktor, in silence, led Dieter around the back passageways of the castle to a door that led out onto the field behind the castle. This was the exit Robert had taken him to golf. If any exit were not being watched, it would be that door. Unfortunately, as they approached the corner leading to that exit, Viktor smelled tobacco and knew that someone, a guard more than likely, was waiting right by the door.

They made their way to a side entrance located directly off the courtyard, which was also guarded.

The blind patient spoke calmly. "Doctor, why don't you just take me back? It's all right. I'm not afraid. I'm not afraid to die. I know where I'm going."

"No, just wait," Viktor said. "I've got one more idea. There's a friend that may be able to help. Come on."

* * * * * *

Viktor, with Dieter in tow, arrived minutes later at Olivia's door. She answered after the first brief knock.

"Viktor! How sweet..." Her eyebrows furrowed as soon as she caught sight of the patient behind the doctor. "What's going on? Why is he here?"

Viktor brushed past her into her room and closed the door as soon as Dieter was safely inside.

"Olivia, I'm sorry to have to involve you in this but I really don't know where else to turn. This is Dieter Himmelbach. Yes, he's blind. But he's not like the other patients. He's special. He's...He's incredibly smart. You have to trust me on this. He's never been formally schooled but he understands physics and other sciences. He's not like the others, but they're just going to kill him, exterminate him like he was just another insect. I didn't know who else to turn to. But, of course, your father's the Director. So, I thought you could talk to him, reason with him on my behalf."

Olivia looked from Viktor to Dieter, then back again. She pursed her lips in thought before speaking.

"I see. So, you want me to talk with my father so that this patient can live? Is that right?"

"Yes, Olivia."

"Viktor, I don't know what to say."

"Just trust me, please, Olivia. Help me."

"I'll see what I can do."

Olivia moved from the room, shutting the door behind her.

"I'm going to get you out of here, Dieter," Viktor said.

"Why?"

This confused Viktor. "Why what?"

"Why would you risk your life to save me, sir?"

"I...I don't know. Look, all I know is that you don't deserve to die like this. Blind or not, you've got a lot to offer this world. It's foolish to kill you just because you're blind."

"So, if I was mentally unstable, if I was insane, then it'd be okay for me to die?"

"No, it's not like that at all. Look, why argue semantics? The truth is you're not mentally unfit. Your brain works better than the

131

majority of the staff. Do you want me to save you or not?"

"Yes, sir. I'd like very much to live. I would just like to be sure that you're not sacrificing yourself for your favorite pet. It wouldn't be fair to me or you, sir."

"Does it make a bit of difference what my motives are?" Viktor asked.

"Of course, sir. Motives are everything. Are you doing this so you won't feel so dirty later in life or is there something else? Do you value me as a person? Is that why you're doing it?"

Viktor looked toward the door and then back at Dieter. "Yes. I value you as a person, Dieter. I think you have a lot to offer. I think you have so much to offer, in fact, that I willing to risk my life to save yours."

Dieter smiled, "Well then, Doctor, thank you."

"You're welcome," Viktor mumbled.

* * * * * *

Minutes later, Olivia returned, accompanied by Captain Oster and Lieutenant Klum. Viktor, who had been sitting on her bed, shot to his feet.

"Olivia!"

"I'm sorry, Viktor. I had to get Captain Oster. It's for your own good. I don't know what's gotten into you. I know this sudden order is a shock and I'm sorry if you think I betrayed you. But someone needs to help you see reason."

Captain Oster, pistol trained on Viktor, smiled crookedly. "Let's go, Doctor. I'll need you to come with me. Lieutenant, take this patient back to the bus line, please."

"Yes, sir," said Klum, grabbing Dieter by the arm and propelling him toward the door.

Dieter stopped in the doorway and turned back to Viktor. "Thank you again, sir. For everything."

Viktor was unable to answer.

As soon as the Lieutenant and Dieter left, Oster motioned with his pistol toward the door. "After you, Doctor."

"Please take care of him, like you promised," Olivia said.

"You have nothing to worry about Miss."

Oster marched Viktor out into the hallway and down toward the courtyard.

132

CHAPTER TWENTY

As silently as Dieter Himmelbach had moved through the world, he exited.

He was herded into a small stone room with a crowd of others. He couldn't tell exactly how many others were with him, but he could definitely hear them and smell their fear. There was some slight sobbing as one of the others came to a realization of their fate, but covering all was silence as the patients filed in and lay on the floor just as they were ordered.

The reason why they were to lie on the floor of this stone-lined floor was cryptic and inconsequential to most of the patients. If the Staff told you to lie on the floor before you boarded a bus, you did what the staff told you to do. No questions were asked. No objections were made. Those who threw a fit were punished immediately.

Dieter reflected that most of the patients would enter eternity no wiser than when they left earth. One day would slip into another. And, he guessed, that would be just fine for most. After all, there was no future for most of them, only the day in and day out routine. There was only what today offered.

He lay down on the cold stone floor and thought of his mother and brother. Dieter had no idea where or what they were doing. He didn't even know if they were still alive. If they were, his brother would be in the military and his mother, well, who really knew where his mother would be.

At the very least he could think about this new family God had given him temporarily. There was Martin, as rough and volatile as a sheet of sandpaper and yet brotherly to the point of sacrifice.

And then there was Doctor Gottlieb. Dieter honestly didn't know what to think about that one.

There was a roar from outside the room as a truck started up.

Dieter would like to think that the two had become friends of a sort. But he couldn't tell. It seemed like the doctor had tried to save him there at the end. But was he trying to save the patient because he cherished their friendship, or because Dieter was some sort of goose that laid golden eggs? Did the doctor really care about him as a person as he said? It had almost seemed like he did care, at the end.

Ventilation flaps in the walls were slowly opened, pushed forward by the influx of gas.

Dieter wondered about the rest of the patients and the madness of the Reich. Could this hatred of anything not pure be kept alive forever? Would the leaders ever face justice for their crimes? Would there ever come a time when those who were less than perfect be thought worthy of life?

The hiss of gas entered the chamber.

I wonder what it will be like to die, thought Dieter. Are there sights not yet seen by mortal eyes? What color will the sky be and the clouds? I wonder if I will have wings. It would be wonderful to be free, to be flying and soaring and dipping through the air like an eagle. I wonder if I'll hear my mother and brother's voices again.

And then he could hear their voices, he could hear many voices all around him. The sky opened and Dieter flew.

* * * * * *

Viktor, now dressed in prison grays, moved across the railway platform. There were no Gestapo present now, only soldier after nameless soldier, armed with machine guns pointed aimlessly at those passing by. Viktor knew none of those in his present crowd. He had long since parted ways with Oster. The Captain had handed him over to the waiting hands of the Gestapo, whose headquarters were in a town called Battsliem ten miles from Sterlingaart.

He had no idea at which work camp he would end up. The guards rarely talked except to move them along, always along to somewhere else. He had attempted to strike up a conversation with a dour, little man on the last train, but the man would not play along. He wrapped himself up in silence and misery like a cocoon.

Viktor couldn't afford to let depression take over. There was no point of it. Being sad for himself wouldn't change one little bit of his predicament.

From Battsliem, he had been herded together with a crowd of about twenty other men and women. They were loaded into the back of a flatbed truck and driven for God alone knew how many miles. On the back roads, one of the prisoners had jumped off the truck and attempted to run through some nearby fields. He hadn't run thirty yards before he was shot in the back and left for manure.

In the next town, Viktor didn't catch the name, they had stopped off at the railway station and were loaded into a cattle car which was already bursting with other prisoners. They had arrived at their current station this morning after a long night of rail travel. Now, they were switching trains, moving along a railway platform to who knew where.

In the midst of the crowd, Viktor caught a glimpse of a man he had shared the last train ride with, a political prisoner named Klunk or Klink. He quickly stepped sideways, between two other prisoners, so he could walk next to the man.

"Hello, friend," said Viktor, "have a good trip?"

The fellow groaned slightly and slowed his step, hoping to evade the doctor.

"I wish my brother was here," Victor said. "It would sure liven this place up a bit. Feels like I'm marching to my own funeral."

"What part of this don't you get? Or are you too simple to understand that we're probably going to our death right now?"

"Be quiet you!" A guard shouted.

In silence, they entered the next available cattle car, moving to the rear of the car. Once inside and out of the earshot of the guards, Viktor continued his conversation.

"No, I wouldn't say I'm simple. I'm just not ready to give up hope."

"Hope? Is that what you call it? What kind of hope do we have? How could you possibly see even a tiny bit of hope in a situation like this?"

"Well, as I see it, a man has two choices in a situation like this..."

"Oh, shut up!" The man said as he moved as far away from Viktor as he possibly could.

Suddenly, a voice in the adjoining car called out. "Viktor? Viktor, is that you?"

The doctor peered through the slats in the railcar toward the next car down the line. At first, he could only make out vague shapes. But then he focused on a pair of pale blue eyes that were staring out of a slat in the next car directly at him. As soon as he recognized the eyes, he laughed aloud.

"August? Why, it can't be my dear brother August Gottlieb, can it?"

"Yes, it certainly is, brother. It certainly is."

"I'm so glad to see you, August, even if I can only see a piece of you at the moment. How have you been? Well, that's a horrible question. Sorry. You wouldn't believe how incredibly depressing these people are."

"Oh, I know," said August. "It's all doom and gloom, twenty-four hours a day. I am glad to see you, Viktor. Also, I may add, that I'm glad to see that I'm not the only one in this mess."

Guards moved forward and swung shut the heavy doors, now that the cars were full. The horn blew several times and then the train began to chug slowly away from the station.

"Well, we're off," August said. He had to scream to be heard above the moving train. "So, I take it things didn't go so well at the castle, Viktor? Apparently being a doctor doesn't protect you from prison."

"Obviously not. And neither does being a priest apparently."

"Yes. Apparently. What would mom and dad think of their two brilliant sons now?"

"I don't know," said Viktor. "But if I were her, I wouldn't be bragging about us any time soon to her church friends."

"So," said August with a slight smile, "now that we've got a little time on our hands..."

"I know that smile. It usually means trouble for me. What have you got in mind?"

"Well," said August, "seeing as how we've got plenty of time on our hands, I thought you might want to discuss the finer points of some undetermined topic. Or, maybe you'd care to learn how to wrestle with God a little."

"Wrestle with God, huh? I thought that was your job."

"He's a big God," August said. "He can wrestle a lot at one time"

Viktor was silent for so long that August grew concerned.

"Viktor?" August asked.

"Sorry," said Viktor. "I got lost in my thoughts. Wrestle with God? Well, I don't have much of a future as a doctor around here. Why not?"

Learn More At

www.lifeunworthy.com

www.ingramcontent.com/pod-product-compliance
Lightning Source LLC
Chambersburg PA
CBHW071959170626
46813CB00005B/1928